ESCAPE

DARK ROAD – BOOK TWO

BRUNO MILLER

ESCAPE:
Dark Road, Book Two

Find out when Bruno's next book is coming out.
Join his mailing list for release news, sales, and the occasional survival tip. No spam ever.
http://brunomillerauthor.com/sign-up/

Published in the United States of America.

Could you protect your own?

Recent EMP attacks have left the country in a state of chaos and upheaval. With two of his children on the East Coast, Ben Davis has left Colorado behind, embarking on a cross-country journey with his eldest son, Joel, one of Joel's classmates, Allie, and the family dog, Gunner.

Very few modern vehicles remain functional, but thanks to Joel's 1972 Chevy Blazer, Ben and his crew are mobile and able to carry supplies. But that doesn't mean they're safe in this post-apocalyptic world.

They soon discover that life as they know it is over. Danger fills every moment of their new reality. No longer can people be trusted. Especially with resources dwindling and new threats around every bend in the road.

Survival means working together but it also means the teenagers have to grow up fast. Ben struggles with some decisions he's forced to make, but he refuses to let his family suffer at the hands of the desperate. Even if he has to shed blood to keep them safe.

Ben's skills as a former Army Ranger are tested repeatedly as he fights to lead his crew across the new wasteland of America. Will there come a time when the dark road ahead is too much?

THE DARK ROAD SERIES

Breakdown

Escape

To Wendy, for all her support.

·] ·

Ben spent a few extra minutes taking in the stars and stretching his neck. Ambling down the steps and off the front porch, he made his way to the garage. He wanted to let Joel and Allie enjoy the power for a little while longer before he shut the generator off. It was a luxury they wouldn't have on the road.

Leaving the house behind along with the extra supplies seemed like such a waste. They were running out of room fast in the Blazer. The house was so well set up with the generator and well-fed cistern, giving Ben another reason not to want to leave it. If they stayed they could survive almost indefinitely. Sure, they would have to be conservative with their resources, but they would be in good shape, relatively speaking.

Staying wasn't an option, though, and Ben knew it. With Emma and Bradley in Maryland, the choice had been made for them. Thanks to his selfish ex-wife, he and Joel, and now Allie, would have to endure a cross-country rescue mission. He could feel his blood pressure rise as he thought of all the complications she had caused. How easy it would have been had she put the kids first and stayed local to the Durango area. Now he might never get to see the rest of his kids again, and Joel might never get to see his brother and sister again.

Ben quickly pushed the thought from his mind and turned his attention to the gear and food he had hastily unloaded and was now spread about in small piles on the garage floor. There was no point in dwelling on what couldn't be changed, and he needed to be productive right now.

But the first thing he had to do was kill the generator so he could hear himself think.

"Sorry, guys." With a glance toward Joel and Allie in the house, he flipped the toggle switch from manual to off on the generator. "Lights out."

The generator sputtered and finally came to rest with a wiggle against its rubber motor mounts. Somehow his task in the garage seemed a little more manageable without the constant rattle of the engine taunting him.

Time to get to work. The sooner he sorted all this gear out and got it loaded, the sooner he could focus on the guns and ammo in the safe. He wanted to keep a spot open for the weapons under the Blazer's rear seat. That way they would be easy to reach from the front seats, and most of what he planned on bringing with them should fit. He could also squeeze some ammo under there as well, with the bulk of it in the ammo cans hidden under less crucial gear in the cargo area.

Ben noticed a light out of the corner of his eye and spun around. He was relieved to see it was Joel coming out to the garage. He had a headlamp on.

"Hey there, everything okay?" Ben assumed Joel would maximize the opportunity to spend some time with Allie and hadn't counted on seeing him for a while.

"Yeah, I just thought I would give you a hand is all." Joel stepped down into the garage and pulled the door closed behind him.

"How's Allie holding up?" Ben asked.

"Good, I think. She fell asleep with Gunner. I was in the kitchen, making us hot chocolate, and when I came back into the living room they were curled up on the couch." Joel snorted. "That dog!"

"He sure has taken to her pretty quickly." Ben smirked.

"Yeah, he has." Joel stood with his hands on his hips and looked at the mess sprawled out on the floor in front of him. "So what can I do?"

"Well…" Ben thought for a second. "You could start by transferring all the food to the duffle bags. It'll save us some room and will be easier to pack in around other things."

"Okay." Joel went to work opening the sealed white tubs and pouring the packets of dehydrated food into the duffel bags.

Ben glanced at his son. The kid was a good worker. "If you're up to it, how about getting that Thule cargo box ready tonight instead of waiting until morning? I'd like to get it mounted on the roof tonight if I can." No telling what the morning would bring. He would rather get the bulk of it done tonight if he could and leave the morning open to double-check everything and deal with any last-minute issues. Once he had the box mounted on the roof racks he would have a better idea how much gear they could bring.

"Sure thing, Dad."

"Thanks." Ben walked over to his workbench and looked through some small metal drawers until he found what he was looking for. He placed the two combination-style padlocks on the top of the bench.

"I'll leave these right here. See if they'll work on the box after you get it cleaned up. They should be the right size. We need to be able to lock it up."

"What about the hitch rack? We can use that to carry some stuff," Joel asked.

"Yeah, been thinking about that. I'm probably going to keep the gas cans and toolbox on there along with some other stuff. Probably limit it to things we can move easily. Maybe strap that old cooler on and use it as a catchall for miscellaneous crap." Ben grabbed a rolled-up garden hose that was hanging on a wall-mounted hook by the door and added it to his growing pile of things to pack.

"What's that for?" Joel asked.

"We're going to have to siphon gas." Ben looked at the Blazer, then back at Joel. "Lots of gas."

He knew the big V-8 would drink down gas at a steady pace, especially at highway speeds. They would need a way to satisfy the big truck's thirst. He figured on using the garden hose and an old hand pump he had. Normally he used it for transferring kerosene from plastic gas tanks to the kerosene heaters he used to keep the garage warm when he was working out there in the wintertime. He could rig that up to pump gasoline just the same and attach it to the long hose to reach the underground tanks at gas stations. Then they wouldn't have to rely on siphoning from cars to fill the 21-gallon tank, as it would most likely take a few cans to get the job done, and he didn't want to stop that much. Better to stop and fill the truck tank and their two 5.5-gallon metal jerry cans all at once.

If they were lucky enough to travel at highway speeds, they would probably get about 10–12 miles per gallon, giving them an approximate range of 350 miles between needing to find a fuel source. Of course, that would include using the fuel in the spare cans, too, but it was still a pretty good range, and Ben was happy with that.

Joel had reduced the 10 white tubs of food to four large duffle bags measuring almost three feet long and about two feet around. They were going to take up quite a bit of room, but at least they wouldn't be recognizable as food to someone snooping around the truck.

"Where do you want them?" Joel struggled with the zipper on the last stuffed bag.

"Just leave them there for now. I'll load them last. I wanted to try to keep the gear below the windows so people wouldn't notice all the stuff, but I don't think we can do that now. I'm afraid I'm going to have to make a few changes to your truck." Ben shook a can of black spray paint until the little marble inside begin to rattle.

"Like what?" Joel frowned.

Ben leaned into the back of the truck and sprayed the bottom three quarters of the rear side window with the paint, leaving several inches at the top clear. Stepping back and looking at his handiwork from the outside, he nodded in approval.

"Yep, that'll do it." Ben proceeded to spray the other side window and the rear window of the cab in a similar fashion.

"My truck!" Joel put his hand on his forehead and slid it down his face slowly.

"Sorry, buddy, I'm gonna need you to take one for the team here." Ben shrugged.

"It's fine. Gotta do what you gotta do, right?" Joel turned and headed out the door. "I'll go get the roof box."

"Thanks." Ben felt bad about spray-painting the windows, but he knew it was the best way to keep prying eyes out their business, and now that they had an extra person riding in the back, he felt it was a necessary safety precaution. Their abundance of supplies would be too obvious, and he didn't want to take the chance of someone noticing.

Ben heard Joel banging his hand on the outside of the overhead door.

"Can you open the door please?" Joel called from outside.

"Hang on." Ben unlocked the door and pulled it up.

Joel dragged the long Thule box into the garage and laid it down on the floor alongside the truck.

"Thanks. I'll get this cleaned up; it's not too bad actually." Joel brushed off some pine needles and opened it up to inspect the interior.

"Looks good to me." Ben, not wanting to waste any time, grabbed one end of the box. "Give me a hand, will you? Let's get it onto the roof."

They hoisted the box up and positioned it on the crossbars.

"That's bigger than I remember. Going to be a

huge help." Ben stepped back from the truck. "Can you get the brackets secured on your own?"

"Yeah, I got it." Joel grabbed the parts on the workbench and pulled the socket set down from the shelf.

"If you have that handled, I'm going to go in and get stuff together in the basement." Ben looked around the garage and took stock of their progress.

"Okay, Dad."

Most everything was now organized into bags or containers and would pack up pretty quickly from here. Before he loaded it all in, though, he wanted to get what they were taking from the basement packed and brought upstairs. He would wait until the morning to load the guns and ammo. That wasn't something he wanted sitting outside overnight, even if it was locked up in the garage.

"I think we'll load up in the morning after all. When you get done with that, why don't you lock up and come on in, okay, bud? Get yourself some sleep and we'll finish up first thing. I'm not going to do too much more tonight. I'm tired so I'll probably hit the rack after I get done downstairs."

"All right, I'll lock up in a few and be right in." Joel looked up for a second and then back at the wrench he was turning. "Goodnight."

"Goodnight, Joel."

· 2 ·

It was unusually chilly for early June in the Rockies, and Ben pulled his flannel overshirt closer to ward off the night air. He looked at the moon and noticed the difference in clarity between the night sky above and the horizon.

Normally, on a night like this with an almost full moon, he would be able to see quite a ways down the valley, but not now. The air had almost a grainy, foggy quality down toward the horizon — enough to make some of the lower-sitting stars almost invisible. It almost looked like there were airborne particles settling into the lower atmosphere. How long would this last, how much was from the bombs, and how much was residual smoke that remained in the atmosphere from the countless fires that were and had been burning?

He leaned against the railing at the top of the steps for a moment before he went in. Looking back at the garage, he wondered if he should stay out

9

here until Joel was done. They hadn't seen anyone on the way up the long gravel road to their house, but that didn't mean they could let their guard down. The houses were so scattered in the development that, over the years, Ben had only gotten to know his closest neighbors—and not very well at that. Still, he didn't think any of them were people he needed to worry about.

Maybe he would just make himself a cup of coffee and wait close by for Joel to finish up and come inside for the night. He entered the mudroom off the kitchen and pulled the door partially shut so it was still open about an inch. With Joel still outside, he felt better about having it partway open and kept the door in his line of sight as he made the coffee. While he was waiting for the coffee to brew on the camp stove, he peeked around the corner and into the living room. Allie was still sleeping on the couch next to Gunner, who took up more than his share of it.

"Never one to miss an opportunity, are you, boy?" Ben whispered to the dog.

Gunner looked up slowly and gave Ben a guilty look, wagging his tail a few times as if he was trying to gain approval. Ben shook his head and grinned as he went back into the kitchen. Taking the coffee off the stove and turning the flame off, he poured it out of the small cooking pot.

He couldn't help having second thoughts. Was

he crazy to drag two teenagers across the country and into the unknown? He had no idea what they would find when they got there. With no way to communicate with his ex or the kids, they couldn't even be sure they would still be there. It was a risk he—they—would have to take.

A deep grumble from Gunner in the living room interrupted his thoughts. Ben instinctively looked at the partially open mudroom door, but there was nothing there. He listened for a second and didn't hear anything out of place. Gunner came around the corner and into the kitchen. Hackles up, he growled again and followed it up with a low grumble of a bark. He focused his attention toward the door, stealing glances at Ben in between protesting growls. This was enough to convince Ben there was something—or someone—outside.

Gunner had been known to bark at a mule deer or two crossing through the property. It wasn't an uncommon thing to happen at their house; in fact, he had even once chased a small black bear to the edge of the yard. Afraid the bear would decide to stop and stand its ground at any moment, Ben and Joel had frantically yelled from the porch to try to get Gunner to stop the chase. All Ben could think of was having to run him into town to the vet to get stitched up from a fight with a bear. Fortunately, Gunner decided to heed their calls and stopped the pursuit.

Gunner was acting differently this time, though, and Ben took notice. He quickly checked back in the other room and saw that Allie was still sleeping before he and Gunner cautiously made their way onto the deck. Just then, Joel wandered out of the garage, pulling the door closed with an unfortunate *thud* before locking it.

"Joel!" Ben said as loud as he could without breaking a whisper. Joel spun around to see his dad with his left hand up to his face, finger pressed against his lips.

"What?" Joel whispered.

"I don't know if it's anything, but Gunner's not happy. Did you hear anything out here?" Ben asked.

"No, I just finished up in the garage and was coming in for the night. It's all locked up." Joel looked back at the garage, double-checking the door he had just locked.

Ben pulled his Glock out and came down the steps toward Joel. Gunner was right behind him, silently working the cool night air with his nose. Walking around outside his own house with the pistol drawn, Ben felt foolish for a split-second. Was he being paranoid? It was probably just some poor critter. Still, though, after the day they had in town, he wasn't taking any chances. He quickly regained his senses, shaking off the notion he was overreacting, and held the gun firm.

"Where's your gun?" Ben looked at Joel and then

turned his attention back to their surroundings. Joel put his hand to his waistband and clenched his teeth, making a sheepish grin.

"I…ah…left it inside." Joel looked down.

"Joel, I thought I told you to keep it with you at all times." Ben clenched his jaw.

"Well, you're no use to me out here then, are you? Get your butt inside—quietly." Ben nodded toward the house and silently slid past Joel without making eye contact. He continued down the outside of the garage wall toward the end of the building.

"Yes sir." Head down, Joel turned away from Ben and snuck inside promptly.

"That kid sometimes, I swear." Ben looked down at Gunner, who was by his side, but the dog was too focused on what he heard earlier to even look up at Ben.

He felt guilty for coming down on the boy so hard, but he had to hold him accountable, now more than ever. They were potentially dealing with life and death situations here. Joel was going to have to learn to take what he said at face value and follow his instructions to the tee if they were going to make it. It was too easy to make a mistake or get caught off guard as Ben knew all too well. It only took a split-second of poor judgment. He'd seen too many young men sent home in a box because they had grown careless, and he had no tolerance for apathy.

With Gunner shadowing less than a foot away, Ben continued to the edge of the building. Stopping at the end of the wall, Ben looked around the corner and down the driveway. The dim moonlight barely provided enough light to see all the way to the end, some 80 yards away.

"Nothing." Careful to stay concealed in the shadow the building cast out over the driveway, Ben deliberately moved to the front side of the garage.

"What do you think, boy? I don't see anything." Ben was about to head back to the house and do a perimeter check there when Gunner stiffened up and tilted his head to the side.

"What is it?"

Just then, a black-tailed jackrabbit bounced out of the scrub brush and landed less than 20 feet away in the middle of the driveway. Ben was surprised at Gunner's composure, given the opportunity literally sitting right in front of him. Ben had witnessed Gunner chase many a rabbit around the yard until exhaustion. To Ben's knowledge, he had never caught one. That didn't seem to stop him from trying, though, but not this time. Instead, the dog didn't budge and stood there motionless, seemingly focused beyond the rabbit.

The rabbit sat up on its hind legs, moving its ears like two mini radar dishes straining to pick up a signal. Suddenly, out of the brush a coyote exploded onto the moonlit driveway and ran full-tilt for the rabbit—and them! Before Ben had a chance to process what was happening, two more coyotes fell in behind the lead dog in a full sprint.

Gunner took two short steps toward the intruders and blasted a few thunderous barks in their direction. The lead coyote, realizing the error of his ways, hit the brakes hard in a cloud of dust and gravel, then scampered back to a protected position behind the other two. The second and third coyotes now stood side by side about 30 feet away. With the rabbit long gone now, they focused their attention on Gunner. Snarling with their teeth barred, both began to advance. Gunner returned the sentiment and began moving toward them.

Ben had to intercede. Gunner could handle one of the coyotes without any problem. He outweighed the 35-pound animals by at least 50 pounds, and one-on-one it would be no contest. Three against one was a different story entirely, however, and they would work as a pack to bring Gunner down. Ben stepped out of the shadows, exposing his six-foot-three frame to the pack of dogs. Rejoined by the original animal, the pack was three strong again. They stopped closing in when they originally saw Ben, but they weren't giving up any ground, at least not as fast as he hoped they would.

Over the years, Ben had a few run-ins with coyotes in the wild and once in town of all places.

The encounters had always gone uneventfully and ended peacefully with the coyote ultimately slinking away. They were generally timid by nature on their own and in small numbers. So why were these three so hell-bent on blood tonight? Had the animals gone crazy too like the looters in town?

He didn't have to wonder for long what was driving them to this level of aggression as he heard the other members of the pack chime in. Their high-pitched howls and cackling taunted them from a not too distant location in the woods off to their left. Ben switched on his headlamp and scanned the woods, counting several pairs of eyes glaring back from the brush. From what he could see and the racket they were making, Ben figured there must have been at least another dozen waiting in the wings to back up the advances of the three.

Ben needed to get this under control—and fast.

"Gunner, heel up!" Ben huffed, keeping his gun trained on the lead dog. Gunner knew this command well from duck hunting, and he swiftly closed in tight to Ben's right leg and held that position. Ben really didn't want to fire a shot and advertise their location, but he saw no other way out of this. It would be hard for anyone to pinpoint a single shot in the mountains, so maybe he could scare them off with just one round if he could intimidate the leader.

He aimed a little to the left of the alpha's head and squeezed off a round into a nearby tree stump. The explosion drowned out the dog's calls immediately and was followed by an intense flash of light and flame that leapt from the barrel, cutting the darkness like a knife for a split-second. If the sound and flame wasn't enough to convince the coyotes to seek their fun elsewhere, the shower of wood splinters and dirt from the tree stump was. Their confidence shaken to the point of retreat, the leader quickly turned and ran with its tail tucked. The remaining dogs followed obediently, disappearing one by one into the shadows from which they had emerged. Within a matter of seconds, silence had reclaimed the night, and the chaos was over.

Ben was glad he didn't have to kill any of the animals, but he was even more satisfied that he resolved the incident with only one shot.

"If only people were that easy to deal with," Ben remarked to Gunner as he thought about the two guys he had to contend with in town earlier.

Gunner looked unfazed by the incident, and other than sniffing around where the coyotes had been and relieving himself on a nearby tree, he seemed satisfied to follow Ben on a quick perimeter check of the house before heading back in.

· 3 ·

Ben was sure to lock the door behind him, and he sat on a small bench in the mudroom to take his boots off.

"What happened?" Joel stuck his head around the corner.

"Coyotes. Quite a few of them actually, acting really aggressive. Never seen them like that before," Ben said without looking up. "They were after a rabbit, I think, until they saw Gunner." The big brown dog wagged his tail at the sound of his name and looked at Ben.

"I scared them off with a warning shot into a stump, and they left pretty quickly." Ben scratched Gunner behind his ear.

"Dad, I'm sorry. I mean...about the gun. I just didn't think to carry it around the house. I mean, our own house. I didn't think..." Joel shrugged.

"No, listen, I'm sorry I came down on you too hard. I just need you to know that things are different now. And until things change, which could be a while, you need to be prepared for almost anything at all times. There are no more guarantees with anything that we used to take for granted." Ben stopped himself at the risk of sounding like he was lecturing Joel. He was sure the boy already felt bad about what had happened.

"Well, I'm sorry anyways. I'm trying to get better at stuff like that, Dad. I really am."

"Don't beat yourself up over it. It's a process and a mindset that you have to get into. You'll develop better habits with time." Ben grabbed Joel's shoulder and used it to pull himself up from his seat.

He had to keep moving. It was getting late, and he still wanted to go through the safe and a few other things in the basement. Looking down at his watch, he checked the time: nine o'clock already.

"Where's Allie? Still sleeping?" Ben asked.

"Yeah, can you believe it?" Joel answered back.

"I can actually. I don't think that girl has had any real sleep since all this began a couple days ago. I'm sure she's mentally and physically wiped out." Ben walked into the kitchen and fired up the mini stove so he could reheat the cup of coffee that he had been pulled away from earlier.

"You should try to get some rest as well, bud. There'll be plenty to do in the morning."

"Yep, on my way." Joel held his headlamp in his

hand and turned it on, shining it up the stairs ahead of him.

"Good night, Joel. Love you!"

"Love you too, Dad. Good night." Joel lazily ascended the steps to his room and disappeared out of sight.

Poor kids, Ben thought to himself. This was really taking a toll on them both. Hopefully the next couple days would be calm and uneventful. He knew better than to think that would be the case, though. He dipped the tip of his finger into the coffee. Hot enough. Pouring the coffee back into the mug from the small pot, he headed to the basement.

On the way, he noticed that Gunner had taken the liberty of resuming his position on the couch with Allie. Ben shook his head and smiled, thinking how glad he was that Gunner hadn't gotten into a tangle with one of the coyotes and that the situation had been defused so easily.

He held the battery-powered LED lantern slightly above his head on the way down the stairs. With his coffee cup in the other hand, he headed straight to the workbench, where he hung the lantern on a nail protruding from a high shelf and set his mug down.

Unlike the garage, where they had hastily unloaded gear from the truck into piles on the floor, the basement was well organized. He knew how much of everything he had and where it was. It wouldn't take too long to put together their load-out. The hardest part would be choosing what to leave behind.

He dialed in the combination to the oversized gun safe and swung the heavy door all the way open. Stepping back, he took a deep breath and exhaled slowly before he began heaving out the heavy ammo cans and lugging them over near to the bottom of the stairs. He would pile everything up here and get Joel to help him carry it up to the truck in the morning. There was no way he was going to leave this stuff in the garage overnight.

With almost all the ammo cans moved, Ben grabbed the last one and lifted it with ease. At first, he thought it was empty, but then suddenly he remembered that he had stored a couple of Uniden GMR 5088 two-way radios. How could he have forgotten about these? They were chargeable through a dock and two rechargeable AA batteries, but he could easily swap them out for regular AA batteries.

He pulled one of the palm-sized units out of the ammo can and looked it over. They had proven handy when he and Joel went snowboarding or skiing over at Wolf Creek. It was common to get separated in the back-country areas of the resort, where cell phone service was limited. These had a range of 50 miles. Although that was reduced by the mountains quite a bit, they were still good for a few miles. They were also waterproof, down to three feet supposedly, although he had never tested that. They even came with a little headset for hands-free use.

He wondered if the ammo can or even the safe had insulated the two radios from the EMP and created a Faraday cage effect. Ben had learned a little about this in the Army, and it was possible that these two radios would still work. As he understood it, a Faraday cage or shield, sometimes also called a Faraday box, was any type of sealed enclosure with an electrically conductive outer layer. It worked by reflecting, absorbing, or opposing any incoming energy fields. Best-case scenario, they'd be able to pick up something from one of the many emergency advisory radio stations across the country, even if they could only get the NOAA frequency. Someone had to be operational.

He knew the government had been ramping up its capabilities to deal with an EMP attack for years. Of course, he also knew they would be reluctant to share information via radio to the general public. Their first priority would be to secure the president in the PEOC (Presidential Emergency Operations Center), believed to be located under the east wing of the White House. Officials could communicate and coordinate with other government entities from the PEOC. Basically, it was a communications bunker and potential evacuation point for the president and staff.

Ben pulled a small cardboard box off a plastic shelving unit in the corner of the room and hurriedly unwrapped a new box of AA batteries. He fumbled with the small batteries as he swapped them out for the battery pack in the radio and turned it on. Leaning forward, he listened eagerly as he used the scan function and watched the display scroll through the channels. Ben watched with disappointment as the little radio zipped up to channel 40 and then started over at channel 1 with the same result each time. Nothing. It hesitated twice at channel 9 but only produced faint static. Ben knew that was the preferred channel for emergency information, but nothing was coming in.

"Crap," he muttered under his breath. He let out a big sigh and turned the radio off, putting it back in the ammo can and throwing all the batteries in with them. Maybe they could pick up a broadcast signal after they got out of the mountains tomorrow. It would have been nice to have a little info before they traveled. Adding the can to the pile by the stairs, he turned his attention back to the safe.

· 4 ·

The first gun he went for was a pistol tucked into one of the door pockets, although the Desert Eagle .50 AE caliber handgun barely fit into the elastic pocket and stretched it to the limit. The .50 AE (Action Express) round was one of the most powerful pistol cartridges in production and at 300 grains would travel over 1,500 feet per second. The pistol weighed in at just under five pounds, even with the seven-round magazine empty. And with an overall length of almost one foot, it wasn't a gun one carried casually. Ben had taken this as his sidearm for protection from predators on a few of their elk-hunting trips, as the gun easily had enough power to stop a charging bear. He didn't shoot it very often at the range, though, with the bullets costing upward of $1.50 each. It didn't see much use and as a result spent most of its time in the safe. Ben stuffed it into an old leather holster and laid it on top of the stacked ammo cans.

The next gun he grabbed was an obvious choice. It was a duplicate of the Olympic AR he had used in town today, except this one was a simplified version with a fixed-front site tower and a flip-up rear sight. He had over a thousand rounds of the 5.56 caliber ammo that they both used. It was also widely available and a common round. He had also acquired about a dozen 30-round magazines over the years and one 60-round novelty magazine that he had only used a few times when they were fooling around at the range. The two guns also featured the same key-mod rail system, so the accessories and sights were interchangeable. The AR was an excellent weapon choice for medium- to close-range combat. In the morning, he could stash it in the tactical gun bag with the other AR upstairs.

Reaching back into the far corner of the safe, he pulled out his Remington M24. This was his primary hunting rifle when they went for elk or mule deer, and it had the longest range of any of his guns while also being the most accurate. Chambered to fire a .338 Lapua Magnum round, it was capable of reaching out beyond 1,500 yards. Ben became familiar with this rifle and learned to use it well while in the service. The Army referred to the gun as a "weapons system" because the 10 × 42 mm scope to be quickly detached and used as a monocular. It also had a bipod attached for stability, like one of the ARs. He slid it into a soft case with a sling and zipped it up.

Leaning the rifle against the growing pile of gear to take, he looked back at the safe. There were still a few other guns in there, although he wasn't sure how many more of them would make the cut. There were a couple of older wooden stocked 22 rifles. One had been Ben's when he was a kid and the other was a little Davey Cricket youth model that Joel had learned to shoot with.

Then there was Joel's .308 Savage hunting rifle. It was the first gun he had saved up for and bought on his own. Ben remembered how proud 12-year-old Joel was when he walked out of the gun shop that day. He took his first deer with that gun and still used it to hunt with.

His and Joel's camouflage shotguns for duck hunting were also in there, next to each other, Joel's 20-gauge Weatherby semiauto, and his 12-gauge Browning semiauto. The sight of those guns alone was enough to drive Gunner into a frenzy. He knew the guns and gear involved in going for ducks and nearly burst with excitement whenever they started getting ready for an outing. Gunner was a quick study and didn't require much training to figure out his role as retriever. He seemed happiest when he was in the water and working the downed birds.

There were also a few guns in there that had

been Ben's fathers: an old double-barrel 12-gauge and a .30-30 lever-action Winchester were among the more notable firearms remaining along the back wall of the safe.

Ben didn't have the heart to follow through on his original plan about the old 12-gauge double-barrel shotgun. At well over a hundred years old, it was an antique at this point, and now that it stood in front of him, he couldn't bear the thought of modifying it. He had thought about cutting down the barrel and the stock and making a compact mini cannon out of the thing.

Not willing to operate on the old gun, he pulled Joel's Weatherby out and gave it a look. Maybe this was a better candidate. It immediately made more sense to Ben for a few reasons. If the need arose, Allie could handle this gun. It was lightweight and could hold twice the amount of ammo as the old shotgun. The wide shot pattern of the number 2 bird shot would allow her to easily hit any target up to 45 yards away without much effort. Ben wasn't sure if she had any experience with guns, but the recoil on the 20-gauge would be far less severe than on the 12-gauge. He couldn't make it quite as short as the other gun, but it would still be easier to handle.

"Okay then, this one it is," he said out loud.

He laid an old towel in the bench top vise and then laid the gun barrel in the towel and tightened the vise until the two sides came together and gripped the portion of the barrel he intended to cut off. He fished a hacksaw from his toolbox and laid it across the barrel. Eyeing it up with the end of the foregrip, he started cutting a half inch past that. Hoping Joel would forgive him for customizing his gun, Ben sliced through the barrel slowly but surely. Once he was down to the last couple of pulls with the saw, he stopped just short of cutting through and held the gun. Giving it a little pressure, the barrel bent easily at the cut and broke off, leaving a small burr that he smoothed down with a flat file.

He re-clamped the gun by the stock and cut through the composite stock smoothly with the fine-toothed saw. With his other hand, he kept a firm grip and went all the way through. The edges needed attention after that. He grabbed an old sanding sponge and smoothed off the ends of what was now the pistol grip.

Impressed with his handy work, he grinned at his creation. He couldn't help but wonder how many laws he had broken with these modifications but figured none of that really mattered at this point. He used the towel in the vise to wrap the gun up just the same and added it to the pile.

He pulled the crate with the coins in it out of the safe and put it up on the workbench. Picking through the assortment, he separated the silver buffalo coins from the rest and put them in a small plastic tub.

There were 265 of the one-ounce coins, and all together they weighed about 16 pounds. He wasn't sure what they would encounter en route to Maryland but figured a little bartering power might go a long way. Cash would be worthless in this post-apocalyptic world, but tangible goods like precious metals, food supplies, and weapons would rule the land.

Ben was reminded of something the old-timers that came into his shop used to mention as the only thing they had faith in anymore—the three G's: God, gold, and guns.

He finished going through the safe, removing anything he thought they would need for their trip, and packed the remaining knives and specialty ammo on the shelves in his last spare ammo can.

Adding the can to the pile, he stepped back to assess how much stuff he had added to the load and tried to figure out how much more he could cram into the truck. He looked around at the shelves in the basement. He grabbed two dark blue plastic water containers with built-in spigots from the top shelf and brushed the dust off them. He hadn't used these since the car camping trip he and all the kids went on when they were here on summer vacation last year. They each held five gallons and were pretty heavy when they were full.

He set them down by the pile, thinking he would fill them up in the morning with the hose outside so he didn't have to carry them far. They should fit with the cooler and gas cans on the rear hitch-mounted rack. That would max out the rear rack most likely, so he'd better start figuring out where he was going to put anything else he decided to bring.

Glancing down at his watch, he realized it was approaching 11:00. Anything else they would bring they could figure out in the morning and pack it once they had everything else loaded, if there was room. Walking over to the still-open safe, Ben took one last look inside at the remaining guns and gear and told himself that he would be back here someday. He wasn't sure if he believed that entirely, but at least telling himself that made it easier to close the safe door, spin the lock, and walk away.

· 5 ·

Satisfied he had done all he could do for the night, Ben moved up the stairs lazily. Checking on Allie on his way through the living room, he was jealous of how soundly Gunner was sleeping as he snored loudly. Plopping down on his bed as soon as he got to his room, he rubbed his hand across his face and up through his hair. Brushing his teeth could wait until morning, he thought, and he turned the little LED lantern off. He'd run the generator for a while in the morning, and they could all enjoy the last hot shower they would most likely get for a while. He was physically and mentally fatigued at this point, and his thoughts were heavy with the prospects of their impending journey.

He tried to remain optimistic but knew, based on the condition of the roads and even the main highway they had seen on the way back from town, it would be a long trip. He wasn't sure if Allie would be up for it, but he hoped Joel could help with the driving if it wasn't too crazy out there. It would be tedious going for sure. They would have to be on the lookout for abandoned vehicles and wrecks the entire time. Driving at night might be impossible to do safely, and not having that option would add a significant amount of time to the trip.

Thinking back to his younger years, he remembered driving east on two separate occasions. One of those times, he was headed to Fort Benning, Georgia, to report for Ranger School and 68 days of hell.

The only other time he had been east, he actually took the same route they were about to attempt on this trip. He and his ex had visited her parents in Maryland before Joel was born. They were young and carefree back then and had made the coffee-fueled road trip in three days, only stopping to spend the night once. This time would be a very different experience and take much longer for sure.

They would head east on 160 initially, and it would presumably be slow going. It was a two-lane road in some sections, winding its way through the Rocky Mountains.

From the western slope of the Rockies to the eastern slope, the route would take them across the Continental Divide with a series of switchbacks. God's country, as Ben liked to call it, and in his opinion some of the most beautiful views he had ever seen.

Most of the higher-elevation passes required snow chains during the winter months. But even with good weather and clear roads it could take most of the day just to get within an hour of Boulder. He had gone up that way last year for a trade show, through Boulder and then on to Denver, remembering it was pretty much a full day's drive. The road was filled with blind corners and drastic elevation changes for at least the first few hours, which added to the difficulty. Maybe they could make up some time once they hit the plains of Kansas where it was straight and flat.

Unable and unwilling to think about anything else, Ben was nearly asleep when his head hit the pillow. Not even bothering to take off his clothes, he pulled the comforter over himself and drifted off involuntarily.

There was an airplane headed straight for the house. Joel could see the long, sleek commercial airliner careening out of control. It almost glowed red, blazing away and leaving a trail of smoke and flames. It was headed straight for them. He couldn't move.

Straining to yell, he opened his mouth, but

nothing came out but a raspy grunt. It was happening so fast. He couldn't move away from the window. He was frozen in place like a statue. His face pressed against the cold, wet glass.

"Whoa! What the…" Joel shot up from his bed and into a seated position, pushing Gunner away as the dog licked his face.

"Oh, man! What a dream!" Joel coughed as he tried to get his voice back. Rubbing his face, he realized he was covered in sweat. He threw the covers off, anxious to pull himself back to reality and leave his crazy dream behind. Gunner forced his snoot into Joel's lap, not willing to be so easily put off.

"All right, all right, come on, you big brown moose," Joel teased. He looked out the window. It was still predawn, but he also knew that once Gunner was up, there would be no peace until he had been let out to do his business. Joel had tried to make the dog wait in the past, but Gunner simply sat in the corner of his room and whined impatiently until Joel surrendered. Based on past performances from the dog, he figured it was probably around 4:30 or 5:00.

He forced himself out of bed, a little unsure of his footing for a second. He balanced himself before leaning over and flicking the light switch.

Click.

"Oh right, duh." He shook his head and fumbled

around on the nightstand for his headlamp.

"There we go." Switching on the light, he made his way downstairs. Halfway down, he remembered that Allie was sleeping on the couch. He paused and switched his headlamp over to the red-light mode, then proceeded quietly. Gunner was waiting impatiently at the bottom of the steps and started for the door as soon as Joel stepped off the last tread.

"Stay," Joel whispered, cracking the door just enough to look around outside. He wanted to make sure it was clear after the coyote incident last night. All seemed calm. "Okay, go ahead."

Gunner flew across the deck and down to the bottom of the steps, not making it more than a few feet before relieving himself. It was just as well with Joel that Gunner stayed close to the house this morning.

"Hey, come on, let's go," Joel called to the dog. Gunner had finished up and was beginning to wander toward the site of last night's little skirmish, sniffing as he went.

"Back inside. Let's go, boy."

Reluctantly, Gunner headed up the steps.

Joel patted the dog's side as he came in. Relieved once Gunner was inside, he locked the door again. He peeked around the corner to check on Allie. She was wrapped up tightly in the covers and motionless except for the rise and fall of the blanket with each breath.

Joel stared at her for a minute, drifting off in deep thought about how much had changed in the last few days. The line between reality and something else blurred as he stood there in the living room, his headlamp casting a red glow over everything. Boy, she was pretty.

The sound of Gunner lapping water out of his bowl broke the silence. It seemed so loud in the quietness of the morning that Joel was afraid the noise would wake Allie at any moment. It got Joel thinking, though, and persuaded him into the kitchen.

He grabbed a soda and a Cliff Bar out of the pantry. His dad would disapprove of this breakfast, but he didn't feel like fixing anything and he was hungry now.

He headed downstairs to see what his dad had gotten into last night. Switching his headlamp back to normal light, he made his way down the steps. He saw the pile of gear at the bottom and looked over the gun bags leaned against the ammo cans. He unzipped the bags just enough to confirm his suspicions about what guns were inside. His .308 was missing. Apparently it didn't make the cut. If he had anything to say about it, they wouldn't be leaving it behind. For now, he would at least get it ready and talk about it with his dad later. Surely they could squeeze it in somewhere.

He set the Cliff Bar down on the workbench and

opened the soda, taking a big gulp of the caffeinated beverage before turning to the safe. His dad had trusted him with the combination a couple years ago. Some of the guns in there were his, after all, and he enjoyed taking them apart and cleaning them.

The mechanics of weapons had always fascinated him. He often thought, after his military career, he wouldn't mind getting a job designing new models and components with one of the big gun manufacturers. In fact, after high school, he wanted to pursue mechanical engineering and get his AutoCAD design certification.

It didn't look like any of that would happen for a long, long time, if ever. He wanted to be mad at someone, but he didn't know who or what good it would do. And with not being fully aware of all the details involved in the politics behind what had happened, he wasn't sure who was more at fault.

He felt like the U.S. had allowed North Korea to become too powerful with weak policy—if that was who, in fact, had bombed them. Of course, the North Korean government was run by a narcissistic nut job, so he guessed some of this was inevitable.

The topic had been discussed some in his world history class, but Mr. Compton hadn't gone into any great detail. Joel knew it had been in the news a lot lately as well and had seen his dad watching TV more than he normally did. But he had no idea things had been this close to the tipping point.

Joel spun the combination on the dial and opened the door. The safe looked practically bare compared to what he was used to seeing in there. He pulled out his .308 and laid it on the bench top, admiring the gun for a second. He had installed a bolt-on muzzle break a few months ago, and it gave the gun a more tactical look, although its primary purpose was to reduce recoil and increase accuracy. He pulled down the soft case for his rifle and slid the .308 inside.

His shotgun was missing from the safe. He hadn't seen it stacked up with the others, so where was it? He looked back at the pile by the steps to see if he'd missed it.

· 6 ·

Ben rubbed his eyes and checked his watch again. His vision was a little clearer now, at least enough to see it was a just past 6:00 a.m.

"Oh, man." He'd hoped to get up earlier, but he wasn't surprised he'd slept later than intended after pushing it last night. Before he did anything this morning, he was going to have some coffee, take a hot shower, and brush his teeth. As long as they could get on the road by 10 or so he would be happy.

He wasn't going to rush. That could lead to mistakes. Instead, he'd take his time packing the rest of the gear into the truck. He'd decided that last night, thinking he might have missed something in his sleep-deprived state.

He had fought the gut-deep urge to scramble when this all went down. There was nothing more he wanted to do than grab Joel and get to Maryland as fast as they could. But he knew that wasn't the way to do things. You needed to make a plan and execute it. Actions based off knee-jerk reactions tended to end in failure—or worse. And they'd had enough worse already.

Forcing himself up and out of bed, he trudged into the bathroom. Putting both hands on the vanity top, he hunched over and leaned in, looking at his face in the mirror. *Tired* was the first word that came to mind. He started to reach for the faucet to splash some cold water on his face, then remembered no water would come out. He needed to turn the generator on for any of this to happen, so he headed for the kitchen. He clearly needed to get some coffee in his system before he tackled anything today.

When he rounded the corner into the living room area, the first thing he noticed was that everything he had piled up in the basement was now at the top of the stairs. And all of it was organized nearly how he had left it.

Ben hadn't been looking forward to carrying the gear and ammo up. None of the ammo cans were very light, and his back was still a little stiff from their hike home the other day.

The next thing he noticed was that the couch was empty, and the blankets were neatly folded and stacked. Surprised that both kids were up, he continued toward the smell of fresh-brewed coffee. He found a half-full pot sitting on top of the mini camp stove in the kitchen. Grabbing a mug from the cabinet, he poured the rest of the steaming black liquid into his cup and inhaled the aroma deeply.

He was impressed with what he'd seen so far this morning. Not only was Joel up early, but he was motivated as well—and Allie, too, apparently. Maybe Allie was a blessing in disguise for them. If this was any indication of how Joel would step up to more responsibility when she was around, then Ben was all for it.

He decided right then that he needed to stop second-guessing himself about bringing her along. He felt guilty in some ways that he'd be exposing her to whatever they would find out in this new world. Joel was different. He was Ben's child and he could live with his decision under the circumstances if something went wrong.

But to risk the safety of someone else's child was a completely different feeling. Of course, every time he had this argument with himself, it always came back around to simply not being able to leave her here. She might not be his kid, but she was someone's daughter, and Ben would feel equally responsible if something happened to her here.

He heard their voices outside on the deck and headed out. Gunner ran over to greet Ben as he came out onto the deck.

"Morning, guys." Ben tipped his cup in their

direction. "Hope you don't mind, but I took the last of it."

"That's okay. We've already had some," Joel answered.

"Morning." Allie brushed her hair from her face and offered him a little smile.

Ben could see that her eyes were still a little puffy, but she looked much better than she had last night. "Morning. And thanks for carrying all that stuff up from the basement, Joel. We'll move it out to the garage after breakfast."

"Allie helped me." Joel shrugged like it was no big deal. "Just trying to help out a little."

Ben nodded at Allie. "Thanks."

"Sure," she said.

"How did everyone sleep?" Ben sipped his coffee and walked over to lean on the railing next to Joel.

"Good," Joel answered.

"Really well. Gunner kept me warm all night." Allie looked at Gunner down in the yard as he sniffed around.

Normally, Ben enjoyed being out on the deck at this time of morning and taking in the first rays of sun as they crept over the mountain behind the house. But this morning, like yesterday morning, there was a heaviness to the sky, and the faint burnt smell that permeated the air dissolved any notion that this was anything but normal.

He glanced at Joel and Allie. They seemed to be exchanging looks.

Ben could take a hint. He pushed off the railing and stepped back, suddenly feeling like he had interrupted a deep conversation. "If you guys want to get cleaned up and get one more shower in, help yourselves. I'm gonna run the generator for a little while."

"Thanks, Dad."

"Thank you, Mr. Davis." Allie shot him that same little smile.

Ben was halfway down the steps when he was intercepted by Gunner, who had been out in the yard and sniffing around in the relative safety of the morning light.

"Hey, boy." Ben scratched the dog's head for a minute before moving on to the garage. He unlocked the door and opened it, checking quickly to be sure everything was the way he left it last night. Thankfully, it was.

Once he got the generator started, he came right back out and locked the door behind him. No point in hanging out in there any more than he had to while it was running. Besides, he wanted to get a shower and fix himself something to eat.

Knowing that they would be leaving in a few hours gave Ben a small amount of relief from his concerns about the noise of running the generator. He wasn't worried about his closest neighbors; he hadn't seen their cars either time they had passed their driveways over the last couple days.

And if anyone were to pick up on the noise from farther away, it would take them a fair amount of time to triangulate the source in the mountains. By then, he, Joel, Allie, and Gunner would be gone.

Ben went back inside, leaving Joel and Allie to their conversation. Finishing his coffee, he stared out the kitchen window for a minute before deciding to make them all a decent breakfast. The eggs, cheese, and butter would still be good, even after a few days without power to the fridge. Might as well eat like kings one last time. No telling how things would go on the road.

"Making breakfast?" Joel, with Allie right behind him, entered the kitchen a few minutes later.

"Yep, I figure we might as well use this stuff up." Ben was cracking the eggs into a large bowl. "Grab the bread out of the pantry, will you, Joel?"

"Sure."

"Need any help?" Allie stepped forward and leaned on the kitchen island countertop.

"Nope, this is my way of saying thanks for saving my back this morning." Ben nodded at the pile of gear they had carried up from the basement. "Why don't you guys get your showers while I make breakfast?"

With that, they were both off. Joel headed

upstairs, Allie down. Gunner, too interested in the food he smelled, stayed put. It was not uncommon for Gunner to get scraps or leftovers in his bowl, and he knew it. The dog was smarter than some people Ben knew.

He finished up cooking and left breakfast on the table for the kids. He gave Gunner a fried egg, then made a sandwich out of his portion of the omelet and wolfed it down on the way to his bedroom. He didn't want to rush, but that didn't mean he wanted to waste any more time here this morning than they had to, either. He took a quick shower and, after he got dressed, threw a few changes of clothes and some toiletries in a bag.

Joel and Allie were just finishing up their food when he came back into the kitchen. Next stop for him was the garage.

"Thanks for breakfast, Mr. Davis. It was really good."

"No problem." Ben nodded.

"What do you want us to do first?" Joel asked.

"Well, I guess get your personal bags together and organized. Just the necessities now. Shouldn't need more than a few changes of clothes, maybe extra socks, toiletries, and whatever else you can't live without. After that, you can start going through the kitchen. Grab any dry goods we can take with us. Pretty much grab anything that will keep, like rice, oatmeal, pasta, that kind of stuff. I'm not sure if we'll have room, but we should take what we can."

"Okay," Joel and Allie replied almost in unison.

"Oh, and one more thing. Bring your phones and chargers. They could restore power and cell service in the not too distant future, or maybe some parts of the country still have it. Who knows?"

"That's a good idea," Allie agreed.

"You never know," Joel chimed in.

"Would you give me a hand getting the ammo cans to the garage first, though, Joel? I want to start with them."

Joel got up to help.

After they brought the last of the ammo out to the garage and stacked it once again, Ben sent Joel inside to pack his own bag and help Allie go through the kitchen.

"You sure you don't want more help?" Joel asked.

"Thanks, buddy. I can get the rest of it."

As Joel went upstairs, Ben turned the generator off and closed the gas supply valve that came through the wall from the big natural gas tank outside. Not knowing when or if they would be back here, he figured it wouldn't hurt to secure things.

He would do a thorough walkthrough of the place and make sure everything was locked up and turned off before they left. If the power grid came back on while they were gone, he didn't want to leave anything to chance.

If someone wanted to break in and use the house while they were gone, there was nothing he could do about it. But like the shop, he didn't see the need to make it easy for someone to take advantage.

He held fast to the hope that they would eventually make it back home.

· 7 ·

Looking now at the piles of supplies they had accumulated, Ben tried to visualize how all of it would fit into the truck.

"Ammo cans first, I guess." Ben sighed as he reached for the first one.

He began to meticulously load the truck. Stacking the ammo cans in the center of the rear cargo area, he built around them with the other supplies. Next, he focused on getting the guns and primary ammo stashed away, being careful to make sure both were still easily accessible.

After a few trips back and forth from the house, he had everything from the basement sorted out and in its place. He was pleased with how the truck packing had started to come together. The Blazer would be full, but it would be well organized.

After Joel and Allie brought him their bags from inside, he was able to fit their personal things and all the camping gear—along with a few other random items like fly rods and tackle, a hatchet, and a shovel to name a few — in the rooftop carrier. Thanks to the cargo box, he found that they had enough room left inside the truck for Gunner and one person to be reasonably comfortable in the back seat.

"How much stuff did you round up from the kitchen?" Ben asked Joel as he headed back into the house from one of his trips out to the garage.

"We came up with a few bags of food. Not a whole lot." Joel shrugged.

"That's fine. Bring out what you have and let's get it packed." Ben went back out and heaved the old cooler, now loaded with a long section of garden hose, hand pump, funnel, and other miscellaneous tools, onto the rear hitch rack.

He latched the cooler down next to the jerry cans with a couple bungee cords. He had emptied the two gas cans into the Blazer's fuel tank last night. They had about half a tank currently, and he hoped they could get a couple good hours of driving in before they had to stop for more. Of course, if an easy, safe opportunity to get gas presented itself sooner, they wouldn't pass it up.

Carrying a few bags filled with food from the kitchen, Joel and Allie walked through the garage door.

"Where do you want us to put the food?" Allie asked.

"Anywhere you can find a spot. We're running a little tight on space." Ben looked down at his watch. It was approaching eight o'clock. At this point, he didn't see any reason why they couldn't be on the road in half an hour or so.

Joel and Allie started stuffing the contents of their bags in with the other gear anywhere they could find a crevice.

"While you two are doing that, I'm going to do a quick walkthrough of the house." Ben headed inside.

He originally planned to unplug all the electronics in the house but realized he could simply secure everything at the panel box. Opening the cover to the electrical panel, he threw the main breaker, then slammed the thin metal door shut.

After that, he began making his way around the house and checking to make sure all the doors and windows were locked and that the curtains and blinds were drawn. Finally satisfied that the house was as secure as it could be, he ended his walkthrough and went back to the kitchen.

Standing in front of the fridge, he pulled down the kids' latest school pictures. He lingered on each one before tucking them into his wallet. He thought about how quickly they were growing up and found it remarkable how fast time had gone by.

And about how much he wanted to see them.

He sent up a little prayer that they were safe

from all this chaos and that they would stay that way until he could get to them.

"Anything else?" Joel interrupted Ben's thoughts as he barged into the kitchen from outside.

"Ah, yeah, actually." Ben turned, caught off guard by Joel's sudden entrance. "You guys want to grab a few pillows and blankets? Might be nice to have them. Plus, they'll work well for covering stuff up in the truck. We should be able to squeeze them in."

"Oh, I hope it's okay, me adding my .308 to the gear?" Joel asked.

"Yeah, right, I noticed that. No, it's fine. Probably not a bad idea," Ben answered, still slightly preoccupied with his thoughts about the kids.

"Cool, thanks." Joel headed off to gather the rest of the stuff.

Alone again, Ben looked around as he went through his mental checklist.

"I guess that's it," Ben said. There was nothing more to do or pack from the house. Well, there was one more thing.

He grabbed his hefty U.S. road atlas from the kitchen counter and, glad he'd kept the old thing now, flipped at the pages with his thumb. He hadn't used it in a while, instead relying on his phone for directions when needed. With all the USGS maps available through an app on his phone, there was no reason to lug this monstrosity around.

It was heavy and quite bulky, but it contained a complete and detailed U.S. road atlas. In the back was a good-sized collection of topographical maps that Ben had accumulated through the years on his many backpacking trips.

Carrying pillows and a neatly stacked assortment of blankets, Joel and Allie reappeared in the kitchen.

"Here, let me get the door for you." Ben opened the mudroom door, allowing them to pass by freely since their arms were full. Of course, not before Gunner could squeeze out in front of them, nearly tripping Joel.

"Dog! Really?" Joel shook his head, caught himself on the doorframe, and almost dropped the blankets.

Gunner knew they were going somewhere and could barely contain his excitement.

"I guess that's it then." Ben followed them onto the deck and locked the door behind him, the moment bittersweet. He hoped to see the old homestead again, but this new world didn't offer those kinds of guarantees.

They laid the blankets across the cargo area of the truck and covered over all the gear, stuffing the pillows on top. Because of the almost completely blacked-out windows and the blankets, Ben couldn't see into the back from the outside. He was good with that.

Allie climbed into the back seat and was immediately joined by an exuberant Gunner. She gave him a kiss and a good scratch on the head.

"You know the drill." Ben tossed the garage keys to Joel and slid behind the wheel.

"Got it." Joel stood by, ready to close the door as the Blazer rolled out from the shade of the garage and into the sun.

Ben stopped the truck and put it in park while he waited for Joel to lock up and rejoin them.

God, please give us safe passage to Bradley and Emma, Ben thought to himself as he squinted against the glare of the sun through the windshield. It had been a long time since he had asked God for anything, but he was asking now. He lowered his sunglasses as Joel climbed into the passenger seat.

"Well, guys, here we go." Ben glanced around the vehicle, giving everyone the most reassuring smile he could muster before putting the truck in gear and heading out.

· 8 ·

Not much had changed since they had last been out on the road. The car wrecks they passed seemed to be putting off less smoke as the fires began to smolder and die. This wasn't necessarily a good thing, though, as now Ben could plainly see the unfortunate people who had been trapped in the wrecks and burned alive.

Allie had slept on the way back from town on the first trip and been spared the horrific scenes that littered the roads. But not now.

Ben noticed her in the rearview mirror. The blank, vacant look on her face as they passed wreck after gruesome wreck said it all. She was in shock, and Ben couldn't blame her. There was nothing he could say or do. This was their new reality. The sooner they accepted that, the sooner they could move past it. The shock and awe would eventually wear off and they would learn to cope with it over time.

There was total silence in the truck for what felt like a long time before Joel broke it with a question. "How long do you think it will take us to get there?"

"I really don't know. If the roads are like this the whole way, it could be a while." Ben remained focused on the road ahead.

"I wonder if the whole country is like this or if it's isolated to certain areas?" Allie scratched Gunner's head as he lay sprawled across the rear seat.

"Gunner, don't be a seat hog." Joel looked back at them and shook his head. "Sorry. He really likes you, I guess."

"It's okay. I don't mind him at all. He's like a big teddy bear." Allie smiled.

They made light conversation for a while, and it was a welcome distraction from the scenery outside. Ben was glad the kids had each other to talk to, and once again he felt validated in his decision to bring her with them.

The big V-8 was using fuel at a faster rate than Ben had anticipated. He watched the needle steadily fall toward the big red E on the gauge. They had only been on the road for a little over two hours and already their half tank of gas had dwindled to just a quarter.

It was all the slowing down and accelerating they were being forced to do as they navigated the sea of accidents and debris. They hadn't even made Pagosa Springs yet, which was only 60 miles away.

He and Joel had been skiing and snowboarding many times at Wolf Creek, just outside the town, and it usually took them an hour or so to make that trip. He really hoped the roads improved, but common sense told him otherwise. The main roads and interstates would most likely be worse, specifically I-70. There was bound to have been more traffic on those roads when the bombs detonated.

This trip was going to take a lot longer than expected, and they were going to have to stop for fuel more frequently, just to add to the fun.

"We're going to need to find a spot to get gas soon," Ben announced. "You guys want to keep an eye out for a place?"

"Okay, are we looking for a gas station or cars to siphon it from?" Joel asked.

"Let's try our luck at a gas station and see what we can figure out with the hand pump."

Ben didn't like the idea of siphoning gas out of someone's car. Most of the cars they saw were burned-out wrecks. The intact vehicles they had seen were parked at residences, and he wasn't about to steal gas from someone else's car in their own driveway. He wasn't sure what kind of situation they would find at a gas station, but it was their best bet.

"There's a station. Up there on the right." Allie pointed.

Ben slowed down as they approached the small service station from the shoulder of the road. It appeared empty except for a few cars, which looked like they were there for repair, along the side in a fenced-in area.

As they cruised by the front of the little convenience store section of the building, they could see that it, too, had been vandalized and looted. It didn't look like there was much left of any value inside the store. The place was a mess, and it reminded Ben of what he saw on their trip into town. The windows were smashed, and shards of glass and trash were scattered everywhere. He pulled around to the other side of the store to look for any signs of activity.

"Place looks deserted." Joel shrugged.

"Let me check it out while you guys wait here." Ben parked on the side of the store. "I need to find the key to the tank lids."

"Dad, let me come with you," Joel pleaded. "I can help."

"No, just wait here, please." Ben didn't want Allie left alone.

"Um… Mr. Davis, I need to use the restroom," Allie said softly.

Ben rubbed his forehead with his fingers, closing his eyes tightly for a second. He couldn't keep them hidden away in the truck for the entire trip. They were going to get involved sooner or later. It might as well be on his terms. Besides, the place looked empty anyways.

He looked at Joel. "Okay, then. Got your gun?"

"Got it," Joel answered quickly.

"Allie, stay close to us and let us check the bathroom first, okay?" Ben glanced into the rearview mirror to make eye contact with her.

"I will," she said.

They all made their way out of the truck—Gunner included.

"Gunner," Ben said sternly. "Load up."

Gunner lowered his head and then reluctantly hopped up into the driver's seat, knowing that the tone of Ben's voice meant it was a nonnegotiable command. Joel had taught Gunner a few commands when he was a puppy. That was one of Ben's rules when they got the dog: that Joel would have to work with him and teach him some basics. Now the front seat was Gunner's preferred place to sit whenever he was made to wait in the car.

"Too much glass everywhere, boy. Besides, we need you to watch the truck." Ben rubbed Gunner between his ears briskly. He gently closed the door, leaving the dog inside with a pitiful look on his face as he stared back out through the window.

"We'll be back. Good boy," Joel said.

They made their way to the front of the store, trying not to step on any of the larger pieces of glass lying on the ground. The smaller pieces were unavoidable and crunched under their hiking boots with every step they took.

Ben held his hand up, signaling them to stay put next to the commercial ice chest they were standing near. It was missing one of its doors and the other barely hung on by one hinge. The cooler was now empty, and its contents formed a large puddle of water around it on the sidewalk.

Ben continued forward alone, slowly pulling the battered empty frame of a door open enough to slip by. With his gun drawn, he made his way down each aisle, carefully checking each lane. The bathroom doors were on either side of the drink coolers in the back of the store. The only other door in the place was behind the register up front, and it looked like it went into the garage area of the service station.

Ben quickly peeked inside each of the restroom doors. The sharp stench of neglect filled his nose, causing him to pull back instinctively. They were both small, single-user bathrooms, and it was easy to see they were empty.

"Come on, guys. All clear." He kept his voice to just above a whisper.

Joel and Allie emerged from behind the large cooler and entered the same way they watched Ben come in.

"The bathroom is clear. Have at it." Ben motioned to the ladies' room door. "I should warn you, though, it's a little rough in there."

"Oh... Okay." Allie grinned nervously as she opened the door.

Immediately pulling back from the pungent odor, she yanked her shirt collar up over her nose and forged ahead.

Ben gave her points for that. "Joel, I need you to stay up by the front of the store and keep an eye out. I have to find a key for the gas tank access. Maybe you can look behind the counter while I check in the garage."

"Okay. What kind of key am I looking for?" Joel asked.

"It should look like a short round pin with a ring attached to it, maybe an inch or two long." Ben held his fingers apart to show the approximate size.

Joel nodded and started looking under the counter where the register once sat.

Ben opened the door to what he presumed was the garage, and after a quick survey he stepped through the doorway and into the big room. It was a four-bay garage and looked pretty much as he expected. The only thing out of place was an overturned toolbox with a line of wrenches strewed out in the middle of the floor. He scanned the wall until he found a key rack and searched through the few sets that were hanging.

He didn't see anything like what he was looking for. He'd seen more than a few fuel transfers in the

Army and always noticed the driver had to unlock the lids with a little silver key like he had described to Joel. He was sure the tanks buried underground here were no different.

Maybe Joel had found it under the counter. The place was such a mess they might never find it, if it was even there. He wondered if he could pry the lid off and started to look for something when he heard the door open behind him.

"I thought I told you to stay up front?" Ben snapped.

"Sorry, but I figured you might want this." Joel dangled a little silver key on the end of his finger while flashing Ben a big grin. "It was hanging on a nail under the counter."

Ben shook his head as he walked over and took it from Joel. "I guess we better get those walkie-talkies out and start using them." Ben eased his tone. "Good job finding the key, by the way." Ben patted Joel on the back on his way past.

Allie was coming out of the bathroom as Ben and Joel made their way out of the garage.

"I found the key," Joel boasted.

"Good job," she said. "Too bad you didn't find some air freshener."

Ben chuckled. It was a good sign that she could make a joke. "Allie, if you're ready, we should get going. We still need to fuel up and fill the spare cans."

Just then Ben heard the rumble of loud exhaust, and it was getting closer by the second. They all turned to look.

"Everybody, get down. Hide," Ben instructed. He grimaced, sorry that he had only brought the pistol with him.

· 9 ·

They watched in the direction the sound was coming from and waited. Whoever was coming was moving fast. A small office building next door, which sat up closer to the road, blocked their view to the south and made it impossible to get a preview of what was coming toward them.

The exhaust note was echoing off the buildings at this point and sounded like it was coming from multiple directions. Whatever it was had no muffler at all.

A camouflaged Ford pickup suddenly appeared from the corner of the building next door and went screaming by. There were at least two people up front, and what looked like a rifle protruded from the passenger window. The most surprising thing, though, was a guy standing up in the bed of the truck and hanging onto the roll bar to keep himself from being blown off the truck. He was brandishing a bottle of something in his right hand while he hung on with the other hand, yelling something at the top of his lungs as they rocketed by.

"Did you see that?" Joel leaned out a little farther from his hiding spot behind an empty display shelf and laughed. "That won't end well." He looked back at Allie, who nodded in agreement.

"Yeah, let's hope they didn't see our truck." Ben remained crouched down, looking in the direction the truck had gone. "Stay put a minute."

They stayed in their hiding spots for another minute until the sound of the truck faded to a dull rumble as it sped away.

"All right, let's go. I want to get back on the road ASAP." Ben scurried from his spot and quickly exited the store.

Joel and Allie were right behind him as they all jogged to the truck. Gunner was fogging up the front window and wagging his tail with excitement as they reached the Blazer. Ben opened his door and shooed Gunner to the back seat while Allie climbed into the back from Joel's side.

Ben didn't bother closing his door as he started the truck and drove over to the colored gas tank lids protruding through the blacktop at the corner of the parking lot. Stopping abruptly, he threw the truck into park.

"Grab that and come with me." Ben nodded toward the AR sitting in the soft case.

Joel was surprised but saw that his dad wasn't kidding around. He unzipped the bag and slid the gun from its sheath, then bolted to the back of the truck, where his dad was pulling the bungee cords off the jerry cans and the cooler.

"Joel, I want you to set up on the hood like I was when you came out of Allie's house. Our biggest threat is that way. Use the scope and keep an eye down the road in case those jokers decide to come back. Go!"

As Joel scrambled around to the front of the truck, he could still see his dad occasionally out of the corner of his eye. He was moving around and pulling things out of the cooler. He flung the coiled-up hose out on the ground in a way that made it unroll almost completely. At one end he had the hand pump attached with three small hose clamps. Prying the cap off the tank filler, he stuck the key into the hole. With a jerk of his arm, he brought his hand back out with the cover and laid it down. Not wasting any time, he immediately began shoving the garden hose into the opening.

Joel suddenly realized that he wasn't doing what his dad had asked him to. He hastily turned his attention to the task he was given and scanned the horizon through the magnified scope. Spinning the gun around, he checked down the road in the direction the truck came from. Seeing nothing in that direction, either, he aimed the gun back the other way and then looked to see how his dad was making out.

To his surprise, he was already standing by the truck with the small hose from the hand pump inserted into the Blazer's gas tank while he cranked the handle around.

"Road is all clear in both directions," Joel called out.

"Good. Keep watching!" Ben answered.

"I'm on it." Joel caught Allie's gaze as he was turning back to the gun and she gave him a quick smile.

A sense of pride came over Joel and seemed to enhance his focus down the scope. He really wanted to prove to Allie that he was responsible and dependable. He hadn't really known what to say to her at times about her mom, but he had done his best to at least listen to what she had to say. It felt like there hadn't been any awkward moments with her. She was easier to talk to than other girls he knew from school. From what he could tell, she seemed pretty down to earth, and he was really starting to like her a lot. He wondered if she felt the same about him.

Allie watched Joel through the windshield. She could hear his dad behind the truck but couldn't see him through the windows or over the gear. She hoped he could get the hand pump working so they could get back on the road quickly. Being stopped like this, especially after that truck with those guys in it had gone by, made her a little nervous.

Suddenly, she felt guilty just sitting there in the truck while they were outside doing all the work.

"Can I do anything to help?" she called out to whoever could hear her through the partially open driver's door.

"Sit tight. Almost done out here!" Ben shouted back.

Joel turned and looked back at her, and she gave him a little smile.

She had liked him for some time now but hadn't had the nerve to ever say anything more than a few passing words to him at school. With their senior year approaching fast, she decided not to risk missing out on her chance to get to know him. Of course, she had no idea they would get to know each other like this.

She was still pretty blown away by the fact he had come looking for her. If it wasn't for Joel and his dad, she might not have lasted much longer. She shuddered at the thought of being curled up in that attic all night. Truth was, she probably owed them her life.

She was very grateful that Joel's dad had agreed

to take her to her father in Pittsburgh. Ben Davis seemed like a good man, and he was certainly good at "things," as Joel had put it. They were her best chance—no, her only chance—at seeing her father.

He was all she had now if her mother was truly gone. She choked back tears as her throat tightened, but something inside of Allie wouldn't allow her to give up on the possibility of her mom being out there somewhere. She might not have been flying when this happened. Allie really had no way of knowing. But she wasn't ready to give up hope.

· 10 ·

"Okay, Joel, wrap it up." Ben stuffed the garden hose and hand pump back into the cooler and strapped it down next to the freshly filled jerry cans. He glanced at his watch.

"That wasn't too bad. Only took about 20 minutes," Ben muttered to himself.

There was a bit of a learning curve to siphoning gas, but they would get more efficient at it, especially as often as they were going to be refueling. With any luck, the key would work at other gas stations and they wouldn't have to waste time searching the store. Hopefully next time would be under better, safer circumstances so he could show Joel how to do it.

Ben pulled off his leather gloves and wedged them between the cooler and the jerry cans on the rack. He wanted them to air out and not stink the truck up with fuel. When he got in, Joel was already in his seat and had the gun tucked back into the bag.

"How'd it work?" Joel asked.

"Pretty well, actually. We'll have to stop more often than I had initially planned on, but it won't be too bad. Especially next time when you help." He chuckled and shoved Joel's shoulder lovingly.

"Yeah, I'll help," Joel said.

"Maybe next time I can go through it with you so you'll know how to do it," Ben said as he started the truck up and pulled away from the gas station.

"Totally."

"How far do you think we'll get today, Mr. Davis?" Allie asked.

"I'm not sure, but I'd like to at least get on the other side of Wolf Creek Pass if we can. We also need to leave ourselves some daylight to make camp and get set up for the night."

Ben accelerated quickly once he was back out on the highway, anxious to put some distance between them and the camouflage truck. He hoped to get in a few productive hours of driving, but more than anything, he just wanted to get out of Pagosa Springs without incident. He'd be able to relax a little once they were back out in the rural areas.

They drove on for a few minutes, the area getting denser with buildings as they neared the center of town.

"You see that?" Ben leaned forward in his seat.

"Yeah, it's like they pushed them out of the way with something." Joel stared at the burned-out frames of several cars all twisted together as they passed by his window.

The deep gouges in the road where the metal dug into the asphalt combined with the trail of ash and smaller burned pieces made it obvious that they had been pushed or pulled off the road. The most unsettling thing about it, though, was that whoever did this hadn't bothered to remove the bodies, which were now as twisted up as the cars.

This made the driving easy, but Ben wondered who had done it. He hoped it wasn't connected with the idiots they'd seen in the pickup, although with the apparent disregard for the deceased he doubted it was the National Guard or other government agency. More likely a bunch of rednecks had cleared their own personal drag strip.

The farther they went, the less Ben liked what he saw.

His hopes for a hassle-free departure from town were dashed as they rounded a curve in the road. There, in front of them about half a mile ahead, was the camouflage Ford doing donuts around an enormous pile of burning trash in a Walmart parking lot. Now missing its rear passenger, the truck spun wildly on the blacktop, leaving tire marks behind.

The Walmart was situated down off the

highway a little ways and was separated from the main road by a smaller access road. They were at a high enough elevation on the road above the shopping center that they had a good vantage point into the parking lot.

"Well, that's what they're using to move the cars." Joel pointed at an old rusty yellow backhoe parked near the front of the store.

Ben could see a couple other pickup trucks near the entrance of the store, as well as several people out front. He assumed all the trucks were in running condition. A few of the bystanders appeared to have AR-style guns slung over their shoulders, and even more of them had bottles in their hands.

Ben slowed the truck quickly and stopped. He could see they had even gone so far as to build two bunker-style pits with bags of mulch and potting soil on either side of the main entrance. Apparently these people had made Walmart their new home. He was momentarily impressed at their resourcefulness but quickly moved on, trying to figure out the best way around them.

The shopping center backed up against steep rock-covered hills, and there was no road around from their right. The side streets to their left had been barricaded off with cars and dumpsters pushed into a roadblock at every intersecting street.

There was no other way around. They were funneling traffic directly past them on purpose. From what he could tell, there was nothing blocking the road in front of the parking lot entrance. Ben figured they hadn't got around to building a checkpoint but probably would in the near future.

"Looks like they've moved into Walmart." Joel shook his head.

"What are we going to do?" Biting her lip, Allie leaned forward over the console in the truck.

"Let me think." Ben sat quietly and rubbed his now semi-bearded jawline as he stared at the shopping center.

"The best thing to do might be nothing at all." He looked at Allie and Joel.

"What do you mean?" Joel asked.

"We drive by quickly. We can take advantage of the cleared road and get past them as fast as we can. Hopefully, they're too drunk or too lazy to chase after us."

"But what if they do?" Allie asked.

Ben didn't need to think to answer that question. "Then we'll be ready for them."

· 11 ·

"First of all, I want you two to switch places." Ben looked at Joel. "I need you in the back."

Joel and Allie awkwardly climbed past each other and traded seats while Gunner watched and wagged his tail as he tried to figure out what all the excitement was. His tail stopped and he got a disappointed look on his face as Allie took the front seat.

"All right. Now, Joel, I want you in a prone shooting position in the back. Go ahead and lie right on top of the gear. Don't worry, you won't hurt anything. Face out the back of the truck and roll the rear window down just enough to get a clear shot with the AR." Ben was glad now they had installed a conversion kit that allowed the rear window to be rolled down like the newer-model Blazers. The old lift gate-style window wouldn't have worked very well for this.

"Got it." Joel pulled the gun out and climbed into the back of the truck to take his position.

"Allie, I want you to crouch down out of sight while we drive by. As soon as I tell you we're clear, get into your seat and put your seatbelt on, okay?"

"Okay." Allie nodded.

"Joel, if they do decide to come after us, all you need to do is take out their tires. Don't worry about anything else."

Ben didn't want his son aiming for the people. By aiming low at the tires, he would disable their vehicles long enough for them to make their getaway without hurting anyone. Not that Ben thought the rednecks deserved to get off easy for their stupid behavior, but he didn't want Joel to live with the same guilt he did. He remembered his first time, and every time thereafter, like it was yesterday. Those were the memories that never seemed to fade. If they had to resort to lethal measures, he wanted to be the one to dole them out. He already had blood on his hands and the burden that came with it. Taking out a few marauding rednecks wouldn't keep him up at night any more than his dreams of days past already did.

Ben watched as Joel settled in on top of the blankets that covered the gear. The thought of what he had just asked his son to do sank in. Ben grimaced at the idea of putting Joel in danger, but what choice did he have? They needed to get through here safely and had no other options.

He wasn't confident Joel could drive at high speeds under pressure, and combined with the fact that eventually the cleared road would end, there was a good chance the rednecks would make at least some attempt to catch them. The potential for incoming gunfire was a risk Ben and the kids would have to take. If it came to that, he thought returning fire would most likely curb any aggression and make pursuit seem like a bad idea.

"Just enough to clear the shot," Ben noted as Joel rolled the big rear window partially down. They wouldn't be able to see Joel behind the blacked-out windows, but it would do nothing to protect him.

"Make sure you can reach something with your feet to stabilize yourself. Find some anchor points. We may be making some evasive maneuvers. If you're not stable, your shots won't be worth a thing."

"Okay, I think I'm set." Joel looked back at them as he wiggled himself in behind the AR and settled into place. He was now lying in the prone position and facing out the rear of the truck through an eight-inch gap at the top of the cab. For stability, he pressed his feet against the C pillars on either side of the rear cab.

"You good?" Ben made eye contact with Joel.

Joel nodded.

"Just remember, take your time. Pick your shots and breathe."

"I will." Joel turned his attention to the rifle, flipping the magnifier down and to the side and leaving the holographic site ready for action.

"I guess it's my turn to disappear." Allie shot Ben a nervous smile and began to situate herself so her knees were on the floor panel and her torso bent over the seat. She balled up her fleece jacket on the seat and hunched over it.

"Sorry, it's the safest place for now." Ben lifted the lid on the center console and pulled the Desert Eagle out. He wedged the holster and gun between his seat and the console and unsnapped the retaining cord so he could easily draw it out.

"Here we go." Ben shifted in his seat as the truck began moving forward. Gunner sat up in the back seat and whined.

"Gunner, down." Ben glanced at the rearview mirror and watched as Gunner reluctantly slid back down with a faint grumble.

The big V-8 roared to life as he pushed the pedal down. They accelerated rapidly as they approached the intersection that led into the shopping center parking lot.

Maybe the rednecks wouldn't even notice the Blazer as it drove by. Between the alcohol and the hot-dogging truck screeching around the parking lot, Ben and the kids might slip by unnoticed. So far there was no indication they had been spotted.

Ben feathered the throttle lightly, trying to coast a little while maintaining 40 or 50 miles per hour. The Blazer's exhaust wasn't too loud at this speed but made a fair amount of noise when he got on it.

Another few hundred yards was all that stood between them and the next commercial strip mall just ahead. If they could pass that corner of the building, they would be out of sight and on their way.

But it wasn't going to be that easy.

"Crap!" Ben glanced back and forth from the rearview mirror to the road. "What's going on, Joel? Talk to me."

"The truck that was doing donuts stopped and a couple of the guys are pointing at us!" Joel blurted out.

"Allie, better get yourself buckled up. We've been made. Hang on back there, Joel."

Allie sprung up into her seat and put on her seatbelt just as Ben pushed the pedal down. The engine screamed to life, followed by a violent jolt forward as the passing gear kicked in and pushed them back into their seats. Now more than ever, Ben was sure that having the engine rebuilt professionally when they fixed up the Blazer was money well spent.

"Talk to me, bud." Ben shifted in his seat and placed a hand on the back of the passenger seat as he twisted to look behind him briefly.

"Two of the guys with guns got in the back of the pickup!" Joel shouted. "They're coming after us!"

· 12 ·

Ben took his hand off the passenger seat and put it back on the wheel.

Allie had a worried look on her face as she strained against the seatbelt to see what was going on behind them.

"We got this. It'll be okay." Ben tried to offer her some encouragement before giving the road his full attention. They had passed by their original goal— the corner of the next strip mall—and were now temporarily out of their pursuers line of sight.

"Joel, let me know when they come around that corner." Ben was doing his best to avoid debris left behind from the amateur road crew and their ancient backhoe.

In some areas they had been too aggressive with the old machine and had dug up chunks of asphalt, creating a minefield of miniature craters and chunks of rubble. It seemed to get worse the farther Ben drove. They must have started clearing the road on this side of town before they figured out how to run the backhoe.

Ben was suddenly faced with a tough choice. He had to slow down or risk tearing the truck apart as it began to vibrate violently from the rough road. Joel would never be able to get a shot off like this, either, at least not one that would matter.

So much for outrunning the rednecks. Their only hope was to get to an unmolested part of the road that hadn't been torn up by the idiots. They could make better time on the sections of road that were littered with wrecks than they could on this garbage.

"They're at the intersection!" Joel shouted.

Ben looked back as he slowed the truck even more. There was no doubt in his mind that the rednecks would *not* slow down when they hit the rough section of road. But he wasn't willing to push the Blazer to the breaking point, because without the truck, they were dead in the water. At this rate, their pursuers would catch up with them soon—or least get close enough, even in their inebriated state—to get a lucky shot off at them.

"Hang on!" Ben instructed, slamming on the brakes. The tires squealed as the truck slid to a halt at a 45-degree angle across the road. "We can't outrun them and risk tearing the truck up. Better to stand our ground here."

He reached back behind him and from under

the rear seat pulled out the soft case containing his M24 rifle.

Ben was getting ready to tell Allie to get back behind the seat, but when he looked in her direction she was already working on it. He nodded at her before slipping out of the truck with the rifle.

He had the loaded gun out of its case and was already extending the feet of the bipod by the time he reached the front of the truck. Flipping the lids of the scope open, he laid the gun down across the hood, a place he'd been all too often lately, it seemed.

The pickup chasing them was still a little over half a mile away but closing fast. He'd been right in assuming they wouldn't slow down over the bad section of road. But at least this way the two guys hanging on for dear life in the back wouldn't be able to get a shot off.

Ben could make out the blue Ford oval on the grill of the truck as it skidded and jumped over the rubble. He wasn't sure how the truck was enduring such torture. The view through his scope revealed how intensely the truck chassis was reacting to the surface of the road. Bolts had to be coming loose, inside and out. Ben could imagine all the parts and pieces on the truck being pushed to their limit.

Focusing intently, he brought his finger to the trigger and was about to squeeze off a round into the engine when all of a sudden he heard the familiar, repeated crack of the AR.

POP… POP… POP… POP. POP.

Ben glanced over his right shoulder. Allie had her hands over her ears. Three more blasts rang out from the AR, followed by Joel's voice.

"I got them."

Ben turned back to look at the old Ford in time to watch the left front tire explode. The front end dove down and kissed the pavement, throwing sparks off the bumper briefly before the whole truck fishtailed left as it tried to compensate for the lost tire. It slid sideways for only a moment before the rough surface caught the right tires and pitched the truck into a catastrophic roll.

The two guys riding in the back were thrown from the bed of the truck immediately. Their bodies flew like rag dolls somersaulting through the air and landing with lifeless bounces on the pavement.

The truck continued to roll as it threw off random parts in every direction, until it finally came to rest on the completely flattened cab. The whole thing had only taken seconds but had seemed to play out in front of Ben in slow motion.

There was no movement from any of the occupants, and it was obvious to Ben that all were dead or would be soon from their injuries. The truck, now just a crumpled, smoking heap of twisted metal, lay in the middle of the road.

Their friends surely wouldn't be far behind. Ben and his crew needed to keep moving and get out of there before the rest of the rednecks showed up and started a firefight.

Ben broke the bipod down on the M24 and switched the safety on before he picked the soft case up off the ground and stowed the rifle. When he got back in the truck, Joel was still lying in the back and staring at what was left of the wreck.

"We're going to get out of here, guys. Everybody back in their seats and buckle up." Ben shoved the rifle under the rear seat and tapped Joel on his foot. "Come on, buddy."

"Okay," Joel mumbled. He slid down from his perch and onto the rear bench next to Gunner. He gave the dog an absentminded pet, then reached back and dragged the gun closer to him, all the while looking back at the wreck he had just caused.

Ben watched him through the rearview mirror. The poor kid's face was pale, and he was visibly shaken by the ordeal.

"Do you want your seat back?" Allie asked. "Joel?" There was concern in her voice. Concern that Ben felt, too.

"Huh? Oh, uh…what?" Joel stumbled over his words.

"Your seat. Do you want it back?" she asked again.

"No, I'm okay. I'll give you a break from Gunner." Joel looked over his shoulder again.

Ben glanced in the rearview mirror. Smoke twisted up in the air, marking the spot of the crash. He wanted to push the truck harder but was already going as fast as he could under the circumstances, trying to put as much distance between them and what had just gone down.

Joel took one last look, then twisted around to face the front as the Ford slipped out of view.

"Finally." Ben sighed. He never thought he would welcome the sight of the burned-out wrecks scattered along the highway, but it meant they could pick up speed and get out of here.

"Good shot, Joel," Ben said. "You did exactly what you were supposed to do. There's no reason at all to feel bad about what happened. They brought it on themselves. It was us or them." That was their world now. Us or them. And there was nothing Ben could do to shield his son from it.

"I know," Joel answered quietly.

The road opened up a bit as they reached the outskirts of town. Ben could maintain a decent rate of speed for extended periods as the obstacles on the road became fewer and farther apart the deeper they headed into the mountains. They were making pretty good time now, and Ben was relieved to put Pagosa Springs far behind them.

They climbed toward the Continental Divide, the eastern slope of the Rocky Mountains, and, hopefully, a safe place to spend the night.

· 13 ·

The road changed quickly, though, from double lanes with gentle curves and bends to a narrow, single-lane road filled with blind corners and switchback curves that slowed them down.

To make things worse, it was starting to rain. The old truck's ventilation system couldn't keep up with three people and a big dog all breathing at the same time. It was a constant struggle to keep the windows clear from fog without having them open. Navigation was a bit nerve-racking, to say the least, trying to make decent progress and keep up a good pace when everything around the next turn was a complete mystery.

A couple times already, they had been unpleasantly surprised by an abandoned car or wreck waiting for them in the middle of the road and forcing them to make some sudden stops. Ben decided the risk of a crashing was too high and slowed down in order to avoid any more close calls.

"This is going to take a lot longer than I thought," Ben muttered.

Allie straightened a little. "How far do you think we'll go today?"

"Originally I was hoping to get within an hour or two of Kansas, but at this rate, we'll be lucky to make Alamosa." Ben exhaled deeply, trying to hide his disappointment.

This was a beautiful drive under normal circumstances, but the once scenic route was now their biggest adversary and presented them with a formidable challenge in navigation.

The only thing between them and a sheer drop-off of a couple hundred feet in some areas was a low rusty guardrail full of nicks and broken sections not yet replaced from the previous winter's plowings. The thin guardrail hardly looked up to the challenge of preventing them from careening over the edge if they were to overshoot one of the switchbacks.

It was pretty common for one of the big plow trucks to catch their blade on the guardrail, and there were always sections of rail to be replaced at the end of every winter season. But no one would be repairing the guardrails this year—or maybe ever.

The rain was letting up, but before Ben could appreciate the improvement in driving conditions, they were presented with their next challenge. As they rounded yet another hairpin turn, they met a jackknifed camper that sat sideways on the road.

The camper was wedged between the cliff wall on the right and what remained of the guardrail on the left. The tongue of the camper chassis, which should have had a truck attached to it, was twisted and bent downward. It, along with about 10 feet of the actual camper body, hung out over the edge of the drop-off. There were a few large creases that had formed along the bottom, where it bent under the weight of the front half that dangled off the cliff. Ben had no idea how the whole thing hadn't been pulled over the edge.

"Whoa! What happened here?" Allie sat forward for a better look.

"Where's the truck that was towing it?" Joel mimicked her, leaning forward from the back seat and straining to get a better view.

"Looks like they lost control and went over the edge." Ben put the Blazer in park and turned it off. There was no way they were going any farther unless they could move the big white Winnebago out of the way.

Ben had been concerned about running into a situation like this, especially on these narrow two-lane roads. He figured sooner or later they'd face a roadblock of some sort based on all the wrecks they had passed. He just wished it wasn't a camper weighing several tons wedged between a mountain and a guardrail.

The possibility of such wrecks had occupied enough space in his thoughts that he had come up with a few ideas about how best to deal with a roadblock like this. The Blazer could have easily pulled a few cars out of the way with the chain and tow strap they had with them. He hadn't given it much thought beyond that, thinking it would be a pretty simple fix.

But a camper, and the way this was wedged in, presented a whole different set of problems. To complicate things further, the steep grade added yet another level of difficulty to the predicament. Even if they could free the camper, there was a chance it would begin to roll downhill toward their truck.

"Looks wedged in there pretty tight." Ben got out of the truck and walked toward the camper to get a better look.

"What do you think?" Joel climbed out of the truck, followed by Allie and Gunner. Gunner quickly ran over to the camper tire and made good use of it after giving it a sniff.

They all stood there in silence for a few minutes as Ben looked over the wreck from one end to the other.

He ran a hand through his hair. "There's no other way around. The closest jeep trail I know of is up ahead a few miles. Joel and I have been up here on some of the trails before, and there's no way that will put us back on the road ahead of this."

Going back wasn't an option as far as Ben was concerned. It would take hours, maybe even days, to continue on a different route, and he wasn't about to go back through Pagosa Springs—not with those rednecks lying in wait.

"We're not going back, are we?" Allie put one hand on the broken piece of guardrail and peeked over the edge.

"No, that's not an option." Ben joined her and looked down at the mangled remains of the large SUV that had been towing the camper when disaster struck. There was no chance of survivors.

"Those poor people!" Allie shook her head as she stepped back from the edge.

"What a way to go." Joel was now standing where Allie had been.

Ben got down on the ground next to the camper's double wheel wells and started to shimmy under to the other side. "What are you doing, Dad?"

"I want to get a look and see how bad it's hung up on the guardrail over here."

Since the front end was well over the cliff and the back end was smashed against the rocks, going under was the only safe way to get to the other side of the big camper. There wasn't enough room for him to squeeze through between the camper and the space by the sheer rock wall. Allie maybe, but he wasn't sending her through.

Once he was on the other side, he inspected the area where the guardrail punctured through the thin aluminum and plastic skin of the camper's hull. It appeared to be the only thing preventing the camper from suffering the same fate as the SUV.

The Winnebago had caught its front corner on the guardrail and peeled back the outer shell on the camper all the way to the side door. The guardrail had sliced through the thin shell like a can opener, exposing the fluffy yellow insulation underneath.

The peeled camper shell had spiraled into a neat roll behind the piece of rail sticking into it. The doorframe was badly distorted, and there was a large gap on the frame where the knob and lock were. Ben pulled the door open easily and peered inside, trying to get an idea of how far the rail stuck into the interior of the RV. He was careful not to step inside or put any weight on the RV itself.

To Ben, it looked like the whole thing could go over the edge at any moment if it shifted. The rail hadn't come through to the inside, which meant it was hanging on by the roll of aluminum skin on the outside. A plan started to materialize in his mind.

As he leaned back out of the camper's doorway, he caught sight of a few children's toys scattered about the disheveled interior and was reminded of the SUV at the bottom of the cliff. His thoughts momentarily drifted to its potential occupants and then to his own kids.

Where had Bradley and Emma been when things went down? Oh, how he regretted not making the extra effort to FaceTime them before he and Joel had left to go camping. He had tried a couple times in the days leading up to the weekend, but he hadn't been able to get through.

He thought about the last communication he had with Emma earlier in the week and pictured the little smiling kissy-face and heart emoji she had ended their text messaging with. Before he could force himself to put it out of his mind, he was overcome once more with the sense of guilt that had been hounding him over the last few days.

"Hang in there, kids," he whispered. "Dad's on his way."

· 14 ·

Ben crawled out from under the camper and stood up, brushing his hands off on his pants. "I think we can move it, but it's going to take a little teamwork."

"We're ready," Allie said.

"Yeah," Joel added. "Just tell us what to do."

"Here's the plan. It's not hanging on by much. I think with a little nudge from the Hi-Lift jack we can get it to go."

"We're going to push it off the cliff?" Joel lifted an eyebrow.

"It's the only choice. If we try to pull it back onto the road, there's a good chance it will slide on the wet asphalt and either hit us or wedge itself farther down the road." Ben nodded at the sharp turn where the truck was parked. "I don't like any of the options we have, but this one is the safest."

He hated the thought of sending this thing over the edge and onto the SUV for several reasons, but if they tried to pull it out of the way, the results could be trip-ending — or worse.

"What do you need us to do?" Allie asked.

"We're going to need the ax and the Hi-Lift jack for starters."

"I'll get them." Joel jogged over to the back of the Blazer while Ben looked for a suitable spot to wedge the jack between the rock wall and the rear of the camper frame.

"Allie, would you please go tell Joel to bring the green climbing rope also?" Ben asked.

"Sure thing, Mr. Davis."

Ben looked around under the back of the RV and saw something that gave him an even better idea for how to get this thing over the edge. Instead of using the jack to force the RV away from the wall, he could simply lift the back end up to the point where the center of gravity would shift forward enough to pull it over the edge. He would still have to weaken the spot on the other side where the guardrail was snagged. But that's what the ax was for. This would eliminate the chance of the whole thing breaking free and sliding downhill.

"What are we going to do with these?" Joel walked up behind Ben while carrying the ax and jack.

"I have the rope." Allie, carrying a neatly coiled and bound bundle of green climbing rope, caught up with Joel. "Is this the one?" She held the rope up.

"That's the one. Thanks." Ben got up from the ground near the back of the RV and took the rope from Allie. Crouching down, he flung the rope under the RV to the road on the other side.

"Joel, I'm going to need you working the jack on this side. I want to lift up the back end and force it to slide off the edge. I think it'll go pretty easy, but it's hung up on the other side. I can get it free with the ax, but I don't want to crawl back under once I do."

"Got it." Joel set the jack down on the ground near the back of the camper. "So what's the rope for?"

"I'm going to tie the camper off to a section of guardrail with a quick-release knot just in case it decides to head your way."

"What do you need me to do?" Allie asked.

"I'd like you to be in the truck with the engine running and ready for Joel to hop in. If this decides not to cooperate and should come sliding down the road, I want you to be ready to move the truck out of the way. Back down the hill until you're well around that last switchback." Ben nodded toward the sharp curve in the road. "Can you handle that?" Ben finished with half a smile in her direction.

"No problem." She smiled back.

"All right then, let's get this show on the road." Ben clapped his hands together and rubbed them briskly. It was getting to be late afternoon and the cloudy sky threatened rain again.

Joel handed him the ax once he was under the RV and slipped out of sight to the other side. Using the rope he had thrown over, he tied it onto the frame near the axles using a quick-release knot and left about a 10-foot length of rope running off the loose end of the knot as a release. This type of knot would be strong enough to hold the RV in one direction if it slipped while providing a way to get the rope back by simply tugging on the loose end he had left. He ran the other end of the rope up the road to a sturdy section of guardrail and tied it off with a quick bowline knot.

With the RV safely secured, he turned his attention to the snagged rail.

"Let me know if you see any movement over there. I'm going to start working on it," Ben called out.

"Okay," Joel answered.

Ben heard Allie start the truck a few moments later as he was sizing up the best place to strike a blow with the ax.

"I really hope this works," he mumbled to himself as he took the first exploratory swing at the aluminum camper skin. The blow did more damage than he anticipated and almost cut all the way through to the yellow insulation. The only thing holding it in place now was a thicker metal band under the skin that looked like part of the internal framework. A couple more solid blows from the ax, however, were too much for the thin metal framework, and the coiled-up roll of material fell to the ground. Now free of the guardrail, the heavier band of metal that seemed to hold up the RV sprung back into place, setting a chain of events into motion.

Ben heard metal scraping as it started sliding up the rock wall behind him. He grabbed the release rope and scrambled away from the RV.

"Get back! It's loose!" he yelled.

The tire in the back wheel well, which had gone flat, seemed to inflate as the RV tipped forward and shifted its weight off the back tire. The whole thing teetered on the front axle for a moment and looked like it was going to tip. It was short-lived, though, and the whole thing ground to a halt and stopped tipping toward the cliff. The top rear of the RV left a trail of white paint on the rocks jutting out from the shear wall. This small section of rock prevented the camper from tipping any further. If they could somehow move the RV forward a few more inches, it would be all they needed to get that section free of the rocks. Once they cleared it, there would be nothing to stop the RV's back end from rising up, allowing the weight of the heavier front end to pull it over the edge.

"Okay, you're up, Joel." Ben looked under the back end of the camper, which was now sitting up noticeably higher. He could see Joel wrestling the jack into place on the other side.

Joel pulled the lever up until the lifting bar on the jack was snug underneath the frame.

"Ready." Still half leaning on the jack handle, he looked over at Ben.

"Go for it." Ben took a couple steps back, dragging the release rope with him.

The rock resisted the force of the jack, and so it was the camper shell that gave, crumpling in against the rock with each pump of the handle.

Ben's parental instincts kicked in. "When it starts to go, you get away from it. You hear me, Joel?"

"I will," he shouted back without looking away from the jack.

Inch by inch, the back end rose until Joel commented on how easy it was getting to pump the jack.

Then it happened. A piece of the boulder the camper was pushing against cracked and popped off, flying through the air. With the rock out of the way, the whole back end launched into the air, sending the Winnebago somersaulting over the edge of the cliff.

It seemed to happen in total silence as Ben watched it disappear over the edge. He gave a sharp tug on the rope to release the knot and then let it go.

"Wow!" Joel jogged over to the edge.

"Not too close. It may have weakened the edge."

Ben barely got the words out of his mouth when they heard it hit the bottom with a loud, messy crash mixed with the sounds of crumpling fiberglass and the screech of metal against rock.

Ben caught up to Joel and put his hand on his chest, pushing him back away from the cliff as he looked over. The crumpled shell lay on the canyon floor. Yellow bits of fiberglass were still floating in the air from the massive force of the impact. Allie and Gunner joined them at the edge for a peek.

"I can't believe how quick it went over!" Allie noted.

"I didn't think there was much holding it." Ben bent down and grabbed the rope that still dangled over the edge. "Well, let's get the tools stowed and get moving. With any luck, we can get down and out of the mountains before it rains again." He was anxious to move on and didn't see the point in dwelling there any longer.

Staying in one place for any length of time, no matter how safe it might seem, felt like a bad idea to Ben. They were already going to have to stop for the night somewhere, and that was all the risk he wanted to take.

· 15 ·

Ben untied the other end of the rope from the guardrail and began coiling it around his arm as he walked toward the truck. Allie carried the ax, and Joel lugged the big jack back to the truck and got them stowed away quickly. Before they knew it, they were on the road. Gunner, his head in Allie's lap, was already contently snoring away in the back seat.

Ben could hardly believe they just pushed an RV over the edge of a cliff, but they had, and his aches and pains could attest to it. He wasn't sure how far he would make it, but he wanted to drive until at least about 6:30 or 7:00. That would give them a few hours of twilight to pick a safe spot, set up camp, and eat before it got too dark to see without flashlights. Nothing could give away their position like a couple of flashlights bouncing around in the dark. He wanted to maintain a stealthy approach to things when they could. He knew it wouldn't always be possible or practical, but based on what they had run into so far, it would be well worth the effort.

Ben glanced in the rearview mirror. Allie looked like she was sleeping or close to it.

"You doing okay?" Ben reached over and squeezed Joel's shoulder and gave him a little shake.

"Yeah, just thinking."

"About what?" Ben asked.

"Everything, nothing, I don't know." Joel exhaled a long breath.

"Yeah, I know what you mean. It's a little overwhelming. I also know this isn't the summer you thought you were going to have, to say the least, and the future looks uncertain right now. But don't let this define you, Joel. Don't let the things we see, and things we are forced to do in order to survive, become who you are. These are all special circumstances."

Joel seemed to think on Ben's words for a moment. "Do you think that Emma and Bradley are all right? I'm mean, mom's a nurse, but she's not good at this kind of survival stuff. She doesn't even like camping."

"I do think they're all right, and I'm sure they could use our help, but I think they're okay. Your mom is pretty smart and a lot tougher than you think. She should be able to keep them all in good shape for a little while. Remember, they're not too far from Grandpa Jack's place. He's got that old chicken farm out in the country."

Jack was his ex-wife's father, and Ben had always gotten along well with him, even after the divorce. They ended up talking a few times a year when he would call to wish Joel a merry Christmas or happy birthday. He was a bit of an outdoor enthusiast and enjoyed hunting and fishing as much as Ben did. That always gave the two something to talk about. Ben was pretty sure his ex would try to get the kids to Jack's and hold up there as long as they could. At least, he hoped that's what they'd do.

"I bet they're already there," Ben followed up. "They could walk from where they live to his place if they had to."

"I hope they did. Grandpa has guns. He can keep them safe," Joel added, nodding as he looked out the window.

"Yeah, he's a pretty handy guy. They'll be just fine until we get there." Ben hoped Joel believed that, because it would help him worry a little less about his brother and sister, but Ben had his doubts.

For one thing, he wasn't sure about Jack's condition and overall health. The man was getting on in years and wasn't the same guy he'd been when Ben and Casey had first met.

Last time Ben had talked to Jack, he'd mentioned some upcoming testing he was having done for his heart. He claimed it was no big deal and that Casey had insisted on it after an episode at Thanksgiving, whatever that meant. Who was he to argue with his daughter the nurse, he had joked. If it was serious, surely she would have let Ben know about it, but then again, maybe not. They talked as seldom as possible and tried to keep it about the kids. Maybe she wouldn't have said anything about her dad not being well. It would be hard for her, Ben knew. Jack was her only family to speak of.

"You know your brother has been learning to shoot over at your grandpa's. Has he told you that, Joel?" Ben looked over to see Joel leaning on the doorframe. His eyes were shut tight.

Let him sleep, Ben thought to himself. It's been one hell of a day. The kids were both not only physically tired, but emotionally as well. Ben knew all too well how heavy thoughts could suck every last bit of energy out of a person. Add that to the physical stress of the day, and they had every excuse to be asleep.

He wasn't sure how much longer he could hold out. As it was, he was fighting the urge to pull over and call it a day. He was already tired and they would have at least a half hour or so of setting up camp for the night after they stopped. Today was going to take everything he had—and then some.

The Rio Grande River ran through the town of Alamosa, Colorado, which was just up ahead. He figured about another hour of tedious driving should put them there around 6:30. The landscape would go dry for a while after the Rio Grande, making that a good place to stop so they would have access to water. He hoped to make Kansas tomorrow and was unsure of the conditions they would have for camping there. It made sense to take advantage of being somewhere familiar while they could.

He knew of a spot on the east side of town where there were a few dirt access roads that eventually led to the river and were off the beaten path. He went car camping there a couple years back when he'd made the drive over here to fish the Rio Grande. He remembered finding a secluded spot and not seeing anyone else the whole weekend he was there. He also remembered catching quite a few good-sized brown trout there.

Fresh trout would be a nice addition to their dinner or maybe even breakfast. He'd put Joel on that as soon as they got there. It would do him some good to get out the rod and catch them all some dinner. A little dose of normalcy would boost his morale. Any little bit of food they could find, hunt, or catch would be more important than he previously thought.

Based on the day they had so far, Ben was now a little concerned about their supplies. At their current rate of travel, they would conserve the food. He was hoping to have some of the dehydrated goods left when they got to Maryland, but now he'd be happy if they had enough to last them the whole trip there.

Water shouldn't be a problem. With the filters they had, it wouldn't be a big deal to make all the potable water they needed. They could pump from almost any source as long as it wasn't tainted with petroleum products. Ben's thoughts flashed back to the airplane crash in the mountains they had seen on their hike home the other day. More specifically, he thought about the hydraulic fluid he had seen running down from the wreck and into the water and the pinkish white foam it had made in the ripples of the river. It made him sick, at the time, to think about the fish it was going to kill and other wildlife that would be adversely affected, but now, realizing that it had other implications in their lives as well, the sick feeling in his stomach returned.

How many other planes had come down in or near rivers and streams across the country? Water sources everywhere could be potentially compromised. Could they even eat the fish from the Rio Grande or any other river for that matter? That complication was something else they would have to evaluate as they made their way across the country.

· 16 ·

They passed through the smaller towns of South Fork, Del Norte, and Monte Vista and were greeted with the same scene over and over again: burned-out husks of what once were thriving little communities. What hadn't been burned or wrecked was vandalized or destroyed by looters. It was hard to believe that people would turn on each other so quickly.

Then again, maybe it wasn't.

When they had stopped to deal with the camper blocking their path, Ben had pulled the radios out from the back and put them in the center console. He'd planned to wait until they were out of the mountains but decided to give them another try now out of sheer boredom. Ben guessed they were only 10 miles from Alamosa at this point now that the taller peaks of the Rockies were in the rearview mirror.

He tried the radio, running through the channels in vain.

"Nothing," Ben mumbled under his breath. He turned the radio off and tossed it back into the console with the other one. He wasn't sure if there were no transmissions being sent or if there was something wrong with the radio. Someone out there had to be trying to communicate, didn't they? At least he and the kids could use them to stay in touch next time they had to separate.

Even more disheartening was the lack of other cars on the road or people out and about in the towns. No doubt the looters had driven them all indoors, turning the places they passed through into ghost towns. Ben knew if it wasn't for the kids in Maryland, they would probably be holed up, too, most likely in the relative safety of their home.

Almost all of the people they had come into contact with so far were trouble and had nefarious intentions. And if those were the only types of people that were out, he was glad they hadn't seen anyone else. But not everyone was like that. Dale, the man who had graciously stopped to pick them up and given them a much-needed ride, was a decent person. Where were all the Dales?

Surely there were still a few good people out there?

"Huh, what?" Joel arched his back and stretched his arms out as far as the confines of the truck would allow. He was pretty sure a nudge from his dad had woken him up.

"You had a pretty good nap there, bud." Ben grinned at him.

"Yeah, I guess I was pretty worn out." Joel looked out the window to get his bearings. They were coming down out of the mountains. Just in that moment, it dawned on Joel that his dad must be getting tired, and suddenly he felt guilty that he and Allie had been sleeping while his dad was still at the wheel.

"Hey, do you want me to help drive?" Joel offered.

"Maybe tomorrow, but I think we're going to call it quits pretty soon. I want to stop before it gets dark."

Allie yawned as she woke up, too. "Where are we?"

Joel looked back to see Allie still half asleep, one hand lazily scratching Gunner's head. She was still sprawled out across the rear seat with Gunner filling in the gaps.

"A few miles outside Alamosa," Ben answered. "I was just getting ready to tell Joel that I know a good spot to spend the night on the other side of town. It's off the main road a little and down by the river. It's fairly secluded, so we should be able to get a peaceful night's rest there."

"Sounds good to me," Joel said. It would feel good to stretch his legs a little.

"If you're feeling up to it, maybe you can catch us some dinner after we get the gear set up." Ben glanced at Joel, clearly waiting for an answer.

"Sure, I'll try," Joel said. He was always up for a little fishing.

"So you guys fly fish?" Allie adjusted herself in the seat, sitting upright and disturbing Gunner, who was sprawled across her legs. "That always looks so peaceful when I see them doing it in town along the river."

"Yeah, it's pretty addicting." Joel grinned.

"I think it would be fun to learn how to do it." Allie looked at Joel as she pulled her hair out of her face and secured it with a hair tie. Gunner now sat up in the seat, panting and looking miserably hot.

"I could teach you." Joel shrugged as he rolled his window down a few inches. Ben did the same, letting some much-needed air into the cabin of the truck.

"That's better. It was getting a little doggy in here," Joel joked and reached back and scratched Gunner's head.

"Awe, poor Gunner." Allie smiled.

Joel got re-situated in his seat and enjoyed the breeze as it washed over his face. He closed his eyes for a second and inhaled deeply. Everyone seemed to be enjoying the fresh air. Even Gunner relaxed and stopped panting after a few minutes.

More and more houses flashed past Joel's window. They must be getting close to town now. Would Alamosa look the same as all the other towns they had been through? Would they ever see a normal place again? Did normal even exist anymore? Everything they had seen so far looked like a scene out of a bad sci-fi movie, and he was beginning to think *that* was the new norm. He had lost count of the wrecks and mangled bodies they'd seen, and if by chance he momentarily drifted off to better thoughts, it only took a glance out the window to jolt him back to reality.

But Allie? She was like a ray of sunshine in this dark, depressing world they were now living in. From her easy smile to her helpful attitude, she was a bright spot he'd begun to count on. Joel was so thankful that things had worked out the way they did. Of course, he felt awful about her mom, but it was all the more reason he was glad he and his dad could be there for her. The thought of her being alone, stuck in that house, made his stomach ache. Outside of his family, she was all he had now, too.

He snuck a peek at her as he poured some water from his Nalgene bottle out into Gunner's collapsible bowl. He thought she looked pretty with her face exposed and hair pulled back. Certainly, a welcome distraction from the scenery out the window.

Gunner gave the bowl a sniff and then a few half-hearted licks before sitting back up into the seat. He leaned into Allie, drooling excess water from the bowl onto her shirt sleeve.

"Really, dog?" Joel uttered. "Sorry about that, Allie."

"It's okay." She brushed the water away with her hand and then wiped it right back onto Gunner. "Back at you, big boy." She giggled and turned to Joel, shrugging her shoulders.

Joel nodded at Allie with a grin. "Put your hand up and say high five."

She did what he suggested and held her hand up.

"High five," she parroted. Gunner responded on cue. He clumsily threw out a big brown paw to meet her hand. His paw was almost the size of Allie's hand as he pushed against her palm. Then he pulled his paw down and leaned into Allie, shoving his head down against her shoulder with a grunt.

"Oh boy, he's really hamming it up." Joel rolled his eyes and shook his head. They both laughed and for a minute, life was good.

Joel was trying to think of something clever to say to keep the mood going when his dad interrupted their fun.

"We might have a problem, guys."

· 17 ·

Joel spun around in his seat and saw something they hadn't seen since they'd started the trip. There were people ahead, and there were quite a few of them at that. It looked like they were gathered in the parking lot of a convenience store. There were at least 20–30 people assembled outside in a rough semicircle that seemed to focus on the front of the store.

"That's quite a crowd." Ben leaned in over the steering wheel to get a better look as he slowed the truck to a roll. No one had noticed them yet, at least as far as he could tell. But they were only a couple hundred yards away and it was just a matter of time before they were spotted.

"What are they doing?" Joel asked.

"Looks like they're trying to loot the place." Some of them were holding tools and pry bars and a few had baseball bats.

"They don't look too friendly," Allie said nervously.

"No, they don't, but there's something else going on here. Something or someone is stopping them from tearing that place apart." Ben strained his eyes to make out what was going on.

Suddenly a gunshot rang out, the muzzle flash on the rooftop of the surrounded store giving away the shooter's location. Now three figures were visible up on the flat roof of the store. They were crouched behind the false front that extended up above the actual roof. Ben got the sense this was their store, and they were making a stand against the mob. It might be a foolish move considering how outnumbered they were, but Ben respected that kind of courage.

"See them on the roof?" Ben pointed so the kids could see the three men.

One of the people on the roof shouted down at the crowd. "Get back or we'll shoot!"

"Dad, look!" Joel gestured to a small group of people farther out on the fringe of the semicircle. The smaller group was looking at the Blazer.

"They're coming this way!" Allie blurted out.

A small group of seven or eight guys started slowly making their way to a point in the road that would intersect with the Blazer's path of travel. Ben hadn't noticed any of them carrying firearms, but that didn't mean anything. They did have a few baseball bats, a shovel, and an ax, though, and they certainly weren't coming over to welcome them to the neighborhood.

Ben stepped on the gas pedal and launched the Blazer forward. The approaching people started running toward them, swinging their various instruments of destruction wildly about and screaming and cursing as they came.

"This is going to be close." Ben gritted his teeth as he maneuvered the truck around a few wrecked cars and tried to get past the rioters before they could run into the road. He wasn't sure what they would do, but they might be stupid enough to try to block them, thinking he wouldn't run them over. They were wrong, though. To protect Joel and Allie, he absolutely would run them down if it came to that. His second-biggest concern next to the kids' safety was doing damage to the truck.

Ben glanced at the store parking lot to see if they had attracted any more interest from the crowd, but no one else seemed to be paying attention to them. The crowd was content to terrorize the poor folks defending their property. But Ben had no time to think about that right now.

The rioters were going to get to the road before Ben could get clear of them. There were too many obstacles between them and the choke point the small group was creating. They were clustered together by a truck that blocked all but a small section of the road. The opening was 10 feet across at most. Plenty big enough to get the Blazer through without any trouble, but not with seven or eight people blocking it.

"You know," Ben said sharply before pausing a second. "I've had just about had enough of this crap today."

"Dad?" Joel's brows lifted in concern.

Ben answered with action. He took his foot of the gas and started to slow down. "Hang on tight!"

He then reached back to hold Gunner in place with his right hand and hung onto the wheel with his left as he drove his foot down on the brake pedal. The Blazer slid to a stop, making the tires sing in protest on the dry pavement. The back end of the truck slightly kicked out to the driver's side as a result of the slide. This put the driver's seat of the Blazer closest to the roadblock at a 45-degree angle.

Just the vantage point Ben wanted.

He reached down to where he had wedged the holstered Desert Eagle between the seat and console and pulled it out with him as he exited the truck in one fluid motion.

He left the door open and stayed behind it. He might be fed up, but that was no reason to be stupid.

"Get the AR ready." Ben gave the order without looking away from the group of people blocking their path.

"Dad, more people are coming over." Joel's voice held the thin edge of fear.

Ben looked over to see a few stragglers break off from the mob at the store and start to wander in their direction. The situation was deteriorating quickly, and with each second that went by, their odds of getting out of there unscathed dropped significantly.

"You keep an eye on those guys and be ready with the gun." Ben motioned at the newcomers. There was no time to waste and Ben needed to act now.

He turned his attention to the group blocking the road.

"Clear the road now!" Ben commanded.

"We just want to talk is all," one of the strangers offered.

"Clear the road now," Ben repeated a little slower but unwavering in his demand.

But the stranger and his crew didn't move.

"Looks like you have a lot of supplies in there, maybe enough to share with us less fortunate folks," the man said with a creepy undertone to his voice. He was the one in the group that Ben had his eye on to begin with, the only one that wasn't holding any type of weapon. Didn't mean the man wasn't carrying.

Ben's suspicions proved to be correct when the man reached around to the small of his back and produced a pistol. He didn't point it at Ben or the truck, but he waved it around in a threatening manner.

"Why don't we just do this the easy way? No need to make things difficult." The man with the gun sneered at them.

Ben glanced at the others getting closer by the second. They were coming straight toward the truck, unlike the first group that had formed the roadblock. He decided it was time to end this.

Bringing the Desert Eagle out into view from behind the door, he raised it up and aimed through the still open window on the doorframe. A couple of the roadblock crew stepped back a bit, but their leader with the gun stood firm.

Ben wasn't sure if the guy was mental or just acting tough in front of the others, but whatever the reason, he attempted to draw on Ben and fired the small-caliber pistol as he brought it up. The bullet hit the ground to the left of Ben and by the time he got set to take another shot, Ben was already halfway through his trigger squeeze.

A split-second later, the nearly one-foot-long, five-pound behemoth of a handgun erupted with a deafening bark, launching the 300-grain lead hollow-point round out of the barrel at over 1,500 feet per second.

With the leader of the group blocking the road in front of them only 20 yards away, the result was immediate and gruesome. The bullet hit him square in the chest. Because of the high velocity, it blew straight through and hit one of the others that had the misfortune of standing directly behind him.

The second man went down fast in a lifeless pile on the ground, but the intended target remained standing with a blank look on his face. Still in shock, he looked down in disbelief at the half-dollar-sized hole that went clear through his chest. He managed a step back before dropping to his knees a few seconds later, followed by a face plant into the blacktop.

The others that had helped form the road block slowly backed away at first and then started running in different directions. Ben slipped around the door and swung the gun in the air over the hood of the truck to discourage the approaching group from advancing, but they were already backing up, too. A few had their hands in the air.

Ben capitalized on the moment. He jumped back in the truck and threw it into drive. He glanced over and saw that Joel had the AR pointed out the window at the retreating crowd.

"Keep it on them," Ben stated as he gave the truck gas and quickly accelerated through the now-open gap in the road.

He did his best to miss the bodies as they navigated through the narrow opening, but it was unavoidable and with the windows down they could hear the sounds of crunching bones and squishing organs under the tires as they drove over the bodies. Ben could see Allie cringe in the rearview mirror as they traversed the human speed bumps.

"Do you see anyone trying to follow us, Allie?" Ben asked, trying to distract her.

She twisted around in her seat, straining to see behind them. "No, I don't think so."

"Good. We still have to go a few miles before we get to the road that leads to the river. If they don't try to follow us, maybe we can still stay there." He glanced at his son. "Good job backing me up back there, Joel."

"Yep, no problem." Joel slid the AR back into the soft case and settled himself in his seat before buckling the seatbelt again.

Ben reached over and grabbed Joel's shoulder, giving him a slight squeeze. They'd made it through.

"Keep checking, Allie, and let me know if you see anyone following us, okay?" Ben asked.

"Okay, I will," Allie answered.

Ben knew the mob would likely go back to terrorizing the store owners. He felt bad for them and wished there was something they could have done to help, but it was every man for himself now, and he couldn't afford to be anything but selfish when it came to putting their needs and safety first.

"I'm sorry it had to go down that way," Ben offered. "I had to do something. It was getting worse by the second. They weren't going to let us leave, even if we had given them everything."

"It's okay. I understand," Allie said. "And thank you." She forced a smile.

Joel nodded but remained silent.

But Ben knew it wasn't okay and didn't want the kids to think he took it lightly. "It's a terrible thing to take a life, and a hard thing to live with." He looked back at Allie and then at Joel. He was all too familiar with the feelings of guilt and second-guessing yourself after something like this happened. It had been years since it was fresh on his conscience, but it all came rushing back to him now.

"This probably won't be the last time that we have to resort to violence to stay safe. I want you to know that I will do what's necessary to keep us all safe. This is a different world we live in now, and you have to look at things differently. I'm not asking you to like it or be okay with it. In fact, if you were, I would say that's not normal. Just try not to let it consume you. We unfortunately can't afford to give people the benefit of the doubt anymore." Ben hoped he wasn't coming off too harsh, but it was the truth and they needed to hear it. "We have to assume the worst with everyone we meet from now on if we're going to make it to your brother and sister in one piece—and Allie's dad." Ben was sure to add in that last part, not wanting Allie to think that her destination was any less important.

Allie nodded as she made eye contact with Ben in the rearview mirror. "Thank you for taking care of us and doing this for me." Both kids nodded in agreement as Joel reached over and put his hand on Ben's shoulder. "We understand, Dad. It'll be okay."

They continued on in silence, weaving their way through the wrecks as they made their way out of Alamosa.

Ben watched for the turn on his right-hand side after they crossed the bridge that spanned the Rio Grande River. He remembered it being around here somewhere.

"Keep your eye out for a paved road that turns into dirt on your side, Joel." Ben leaned over in his seat toward Joel's side of the truck. "I think it's called Fifth Street or something like that."

"I see it." Allie pointed from the back seat.

"Good eyes," Ben said.

As they turned down the road and passed several houses, it went from pavement to dirt quickly and curved to the right. Before they knew it, they were out of the residential area and into a more rural setting.

They were losing light fast now. Ben hadn't planned on getting jammed up in town, but he was glad they had any light left at all. Satisfied that no one had followed them, he began to relax a little. It would be good to get some sleep. He hoped the spot he was thinking of would be as he remembered it: secluded enough to provide an incident-free night. But he knew, regardless, they would have to be ready for anything.

· 18 ·

Ben maneuvered the Blazer slowly down the dirt road. It was almost dusk, and normally he would have used the headlights, but he didn't want to risk drawing attention to their location, so decided instead to navigate by what little moonlight there was.

They finally made it to the river, where the road forked to the left and right as it followed along the water's edge in both directions. They took the left and headed downstream even farther away from town. They continued on for a couple minutes, passing by a few small areas that looked like they had seen quite a few campers in the past.

The road came to an end at a cluster of cottonwood trees that ran out from the rocks and down to the river's edge. The official road ended there, but Ben was able to guide the Blazer through a narrow section of the trees. Once on the other side of the trees, the vegetation opened up a little into a sandy area that looked like the perfect spot to set up camp.

Ben pulled the truck against the rocks on the far side of the clearing, away from the river, and shut it down. "Well, this is it, guys. Our home for the evening."

"Looks like a pretty good spot," Joel commented as they all eagerly exited the truck.

"Oh, that feels good." Ben sighed as he arched his back with his hands on his hips. It felt refreshing to be out from behind the wheel. It was hard driving and having to keep a constant watch out for hazards in the road, and the effort had taken its toll on him.

"Hey, you!" Allie had climbed out of the Blazer's front passenger door and was now squashed against the doorframe by an overenthusiastic Gunner also trying to get out. As soon as he hit the ground, he was off on a wild sniffing spree around the soon-to-be campsite, finding several places to leave his mark on a few unlucky trees and shrubs as he went.

"Gunner, easy boy." Joel shook his head. "Sorry, he has no manners."

"That's okay." Allie laughed.

Ben originally thought he would make a small fire and relax with Joel and Allie while they cooked their dinner. But after what had happened in town, he was reluctant to risk giving away their location with a regular camp fire. Not to mention he was exhausted from driving and really just wanted to eat something and lie down.

"Joel, why don't you show Allie how to set up her tent? I brought your sister's sleeping bag and mat for her to use." Ben threw Joel the keys to the rooftop cargo box and headed down to the river.

"Got it," Joel answered.

Ben thought about the fire again as he walked. It was too tempting and too easy to fire up the little gas-fed camp stove and have boiling water and then a nice hot meal in a few minutes.

Besides, if he did make a fire, he would have to use the Dakota two-hole method and make it smokeless. That required him to dig two holes a few inches apart and then connect them with a small tunnel at the bottom. He would build the fire in one of the holes and leave the other open.

The method served two purposes: first, it concealed the fire below ground level, and second, the design caused an influx of oxygen through the empty shaft that allowed it to burn virtually smoke-free. This method was a little more work in rocky soil, however, and he could cook the trout in a pan on the stove just the same, although it wouldn't taste as good as if he cooked it over an open flame. Ben stared at the river. It was probably too late for Joel to catch anything tonight anyway. Maybe in the morning they could do all that depending on how he felt.

When Ben reached the river's edge, he took a deep breath, inhaling the familiar smell of the water. Crouching down and then putting his right knee on a rock, he lowered his face to the water and looked closely at it in the fleeting light. He sniffed at the water again, this time only a few inches away. He dipped his hand into the cool running water and rubbed his fingers together. No smell, didn't feel oily or unusual.

"Thank God," he mumbled under his breath as he put his hands together, making a scoop and splashing water on his face. It felt so good to wash the day off and relax for a moment. The tranquility of the running river and refreshing water was short-lived, however, when he was joined by Gunner, who clumsily wadded in over the rocks and pebbles and began lapping at the water loudly a couple feet away from him.

The water quickly clouded with sediment as Gunner explored the water's edge and followed it up stream a few yards above Ben. Leaving Gunner to his muddy water, Ben stood up slowly, feeling every mile they had driven today in his muscles and joints.

Tonight was going to be about getting some rest so they could get a good start tomorrow. He hoped they could make up for the time they'd lost today due to all the obstacles they had faced. But if Joel and Allie wanted to stay up a little, that was fine.

They had both gotten some sleep, after all, while he'd driven. In fact, Ben would feel better knowing that someone was awake and watching over the camp, even if it was just for a little while.

Gunner raced up the beach once he realized that he had been left behind in the water, and he quickly caught up to and passed Ben on his way back to the truck. He charged right up to where Joel and Allie were setting up camp before shaking off. He released a shower of mud and water onto the kids.

"Oh really, dog?" Joel exclaimed.

Allie gasped. "Ah, yuck!"

Gunner, now seemingly content that he had adequately offended everyone, settled down near the bags and gear Joel had taken out of the truck.

"Thanks for grabbing my tent." Ben saw that Joel had put his tent, bag, and mat in a separate pile for him and had even gotten the little stove out and partially set up.

"A little late to fish tonight, I guess?" Joel said.

"Yeah, I think so." Ben sighed. "Maybe in the morning before we head out we can get a good breakfast in us."

"How far do you think we'll get tomorrow?" Allie unrolled her sleep mat on the floor of her tent.

"I hope to make Kansas if we can stay out of trouble and the roads aren't too bad." Ben began to get his tent squared away. "Once we get on the bigger interstates like I-70, the going should get a little easier."

Joel had already finished setting up his tent and sleeping bag and was now working on getting a pot of water to boil for their dehydrated dinner.

"What'll it be? Chilly Mac with Beef or Cheesy Lasagna?" Joel held up the pouches and grinned. "It says they're two servings each, so I guess we'll make both. That should be enough for everyone since we only had a few Cliff Bars for lunch."

"Sounds good to me," Allie chimed in with a smile.

"Go for it, chef." Ben gave Joel a quick thumbs-up and a crooked smile as he finished prepping his tent for what he hoped would be a good night's sleep.

Allie folded up a few of the blankets from the back of the truck and placed them neatly around the stove for them to sit on. They settled in and talked for a while as they waited for the food to cook in the bags. Ben mostly listened, feeling himself drifting off several times. When the food was finally ready, he ate his quickly and finished off most of the water in his Nalgene bottle, leaving just enough to brush his teeth with.

"Well, guys, I'm going to clean up and hit the sack. Tomorrow will be here before you know it," Ben stood up and shuffled over to his tent. He grabbed a small bag of toiletries from his gear and headed back to the river. He cleaned up the best he could by the water, or at least as much as he had the energy for tonight, then headed back to camp. When he returned, Joel and Allie were sitting on the blankets by the stove. They were still talking, too.

Joel held out one of the bags. "Allie has a little left over, not much. Do you want it, Dad?"

"No thanks, I'm good. Let Gunner have it if you want."

At the sound of his name, Gunner started wagging his tail as he eyed the bag of leftovers. Joel got up and poured the small amount of remaining food over some dry dog food in his collapsible bowl. Gunner buried his snout in the bowl and wolfed it down before Joel could even make it back to his seat next to Allie.

"Someone was hungry," Allie noted.

Joel shook his head. "He's always hungry, especially for leftovers."

"If you guys don't mind cleaning up, I'm going to call it a night." Ben wandered over to his tent and tossed the small toiletry bag back inside.

"No problem, we got it," Joel replied.

Ben sat down in his tent, his feet still outside the opening, and took his boots and socks off, then let out a deep breath.

"Ah, that feels good," he mumbled under his breath. "Good night, guys."

"Good night, Mr. Davis." Allie smiled. "Thanks for keeping us safe today."

"Good night, Dad," Joel added.

Ben smiled back. Then he pulled his legs and feet inside the tent and zipped the flap closed behind him. He was too tired to think about anything as he took off his pants and flannel shirt and rolled them up to make a crude pillow. Zipping himself into his sleeping bag, he drifted off in no time to the faint sounds of the gurgling river.

There'd be plenty of time tomorrow to worry about what lay ahead.

· 19 ·

"That was crazy today, wasn't it?" Allie's eyes widened.

"Um yeah, but which part? The whole day was nuts," Joel huffed. "I mean, I can't even get my head wrapped around everything that happened today."

"I know what you mean. It's all a bit blurry right now, and I think I prefer it that way." Allie played with the zipper on her fleece. "You did a really good job today, Joel, and I just wanted to say thank you. I mean…" Allie wiped at her eyes, failing to hide a tear as it rolled down her cheek.

Joel didn't know what to do or say. He wanted to grab her and squeeze her and tell her everything would be okay, but he was too shy and didn't want to create an awkward situation. He knew she had been through a lot—they all had—and it was going to take time to adjust to their new lives. Finally, he forced himself to say something.

"I'm here for you, Allie."

She sniffled and brushed her hair out of her face, managing a small crooked smile.

"We're all here for you, okay?" Joel repeated.

"I know, and I'm so grateful that I'm not still stuck in that attic or worse. If it wasn't for you guys coming along…" Unable or unwilling to finish the sentence, Allie shook her head and looked back down at the ground, letting her hair fall forward to cover her face once more.

Joel leaned over toward Allie and hesitated for a moment before he reached out nervously and put his hand on her shoulder, giving Allie a few small pats. To his surprise, Allie scooted over against him on the blanket and leaned in, resting her head on his shoulder.

Joel's heart skipped a beat, then picked up tempo until it thumped wildly. He felt like he could hear it and wondered if Allie noticed. He began to calm down, though, and relax a little as the scent of her hair filled the air. It was a flowery, clean smell, and it put him at peace as he inhaled the fragrance and felt the girl of his dreams lean into him.

Joel could have stayed there for hours, maybe even all night. All he knew was that as long as she remained leaning on him, he wouldn't dare move and end this moment. Eventually, though, it did end.

Allie slowly raised her head off his shoulder and

took some of her weight off him. She rubbed her face with her hands and then reached down to give Gunner a few well-received scratches behind his ear.

"Wow, I'm getting really tired all of a sudden." Allie took a deep breath and sat up straight. "We should probably get things cleaned up and get some sleep, too."

"Yeah, you're right." Joel sighed. The moment was over.

They both went to their respective tents and got what they needed before meeting back up to walk down to the river. Joel, his toothbrush dangling out of his mouth, was carrying all the empty Nalgene bottles and the water filter in a jumbled mess in his arms.

"Here, let me help you." Allie grabbed the empty water containers by the plastic piece that connected the tops to the containers, making it possible for her to get them all in one hand.

Joel removed his toothbrush from his mouth with his now free hand. "Oh, she's got skills." He laughed and playfully bumped into her a little bit with his hip.

Gunner flew by, barely missing them by a few inches, on his way to the river for a late-night swim, but he reluctantly slowed down and eventually stopped when Joel called out to him.

"Gunner, no! Not if you think you're getting in my tent!" Joel shook his head.

"Aw, poor guy." Allie rubbed Gunner's head when they caught up to where he had stopped his assault on the river.

"Poor me." Joel chuckled. "Have you ever had to sleep with a wet dog in a tent?"

They set the bottles and pump down while they brushed their teeth and kept an eye on the dog as he drank from the water's edge. Every so often, Joel found it necessary to remind Gunner not to venture in and get wet. Finally, Gunner found a rock to his liking. It was close enough to the river to sneak in a few defiant laps of water, and he settled in with his paw hung over the edge.

Joel finished up with his toothbrush and tucked it into his back pocket. He got right to work with the pump and started filling the first bottle. As soon as it was full, he unscrewed it from the pump body and put the lid back on. He turned to put the bottle aside and got a new one, only to find Allie was ready and waiting behind him. She took the newly filled bottle from him and handed him the next empty one. With their little system in place, they filled nine bottles in no time at all.

"Let me show you a little trick," Joel said. He bent down along the edge where the rocks made a natural bowl. He began to organize more rocks around the edge, making a small contained area of water about a foot deep.

"Hey, look at this." Joel held up a small, smooth

multicolored stone honed into an almost perfect sphere by the river. He handed it to Allie and got back to arranging the rocks until they were spaced out far enough to allow the current to flow through freely.

"Wow, that's really pretty," Allie said as she studied the small stone in her hand. "Can I have it?"

Joel looked back and smiled at her. "Sure."

"Thanks." Allie dried it off with her shirt sleeve and stuffed it into her pocket.

"We can each take one water bottle to bed if you want, but I'll put the rest in here overnight. They'll be nice and cold in the morning, and if we wrap them up in a blanket, they'll stay that way for a while. It'll be nice to have cold water for the ride tomorrow."

"I like it," Allie said. "That's a good idea."

Joel wiggled his eyebrows at her. "See, there's more to me than just my good looks."

Allie laughed and gave Joel a smile. He was glad to see her smile and joke around a little. He was worried about her, and it was good to see her let her guard down. Joel knew that was the real Allie—the girl he would have gotten to know this summer if the world hadn't fallen apart. They would get to know each other now for sure, but what version of themselves were they now? Everything was turned upside down overnight by the bombs. Life as they knew it had changed forever. How could they not change with it?

They each carried a bottle of water back with them, and Joel brought an extra one to leave outside his dad's tent. They looked around camp one more time to make sure they hadn't forgotten anything. Then Joel double-checked that the truck was locked up.

"Looks good to me." Joel glanced around.

Allie approached her tent and unzipped the flap before she sat down inside and began taking off her hiking boots outside the doorway. Gunner sauntered over to where she was sitting and stood motionless in front of her, only a few inches away, making it impossible for Allie to get to her shoes.

"Um, excuse me," Allie protested. "Do you know what this is all about?" She peered around Gunner to look at Joel, who was now sitting halfway in his tent a couple feet away.

"Oh, he thinks he's sleeping with you tonight. I'm surprised he's being so polite about it." Joel snorted.

"Is that what you want, boy?" Allie rubbed Gunner's neck. "Come on then."

"I guess I'm not good enough anymore." Joel looked at Gunner, but he was gone, already through the opening Allie had made for him in the tent.

"Well then, good night, you two. Sleep tight." Joel smiled and pulled his legs into his tent.

"Good night, Joel." Allie smiled back and joined Gunner in her tent. He had made himself comfortable at the foot of her bag and was curled up in a tight ball. She got into her bag and worked her legs around the dog as best as she could without disturbing him. She found some warm spots from where he had been lying already and pushed her cold feet into those areas, enjoying the warmth.

As tired as she was, her mind was racing from one thing to the next. So much had happened within such a small amount of time that it was overwhelming. The feelings she had right now were bittersweet. Out of all the bad things that had happened, she still couldn't get over how Joel and his dad had taken her in and treated her with such kindness.

On top of all of that, she knew she was beginning to have strong feelings for Joel. How was she going to balance these different emotions?

And what would she do if they did or didn't find her father? She knew he was a hardcore city dweller and worked in IT. He was as far removed from the outdoor self-sustaining type as a person could probably be. Nothing like Ben or Joel. She tried to stop herself from dwelling on that as her thoughts began to drift to the possibility that her dad was not okay. What were the odds that he'd found a way to survive?

No. She couldn't let herself think like that. She tried to focus on other things—about how the only sure things she had going in her life right now were the people in this little riverside camp, and she was thankful for them.

Eventually the need for sleep overcame her, and the soothing sounds of the river lulled her into a deep sleep with better hopes for tomorrow.

· 20 ·

Ben felt like he hadn't been asleep for very long when he heard Gunner's low growl from outside his tent. He sat up slowly and checked his watch: a little after five in the morning. He scrubbed a hand over his face. What was going on?

Then he heard a noise that sounded like paper rustling or like someone was trying to open a bag of potato chips. Was it the wind? No, there it was again. It was too deliberate. Ben heard Gunner grunt, followed by a whine; he must have been stuck in somebody's tent.

Ben felt around in his makeshift pillow until he found the familiar shape of his gun. He pulled it out before he unzipped his tent fly as quietly as he could. As soon as he had it open enough, he peeked through and spotted their intruder. A big blue and white magpie was busy shoving his head into the empty food bags from last night's dinner.

Ben finished unzipping his tent, sat up with his legs crossed, and stretched his upper body for a minute. The bird was oblivious to his presence and was fully engrossed in picking the bags clean of whatever food scraps he could find.

"Shoo, go on," Ben whispered as loud as he dared, not wanting to wake anyone, just enough to scare the bird. It took off instantly with a jump and was gone.

He heard Gunner give off a pitiful whine from what sounded like Allie's tent. Ben got dressed quickly and threw his shoes on without tying them. He shuffled over to Allie's tent and unzipped her door from the side closest to the tent's end, where he figured Gunner had slept. Sure enough, as soon as there was a small opening, a brown nose thrust out into the morning air, followed by the rest of the dog pushing the zipper open as he slid out.

"Okay, easy there, boy. I see you."

Gunner was happy to be free from the tent and quickly went about his investigation of the noise he had heard. Ben picked up the empty food bags and stuffed them into the cooler on the back of the truck before Gunner could get into them.

Well, he was up now. Might as well make some coffee. He considered lying back down for a little while, but he knew how that would go and decided not to give in. He was happy to see the truck locked and things tidied up from last night—except the food bags of course, but he could let that slide.

Joel and Allie were both giving it their best effort, and he could tell. The fresh water they left him outside his tent more than made up for it, though, and he was using it to make his coffee.

When the coffee was done, he poured himself a fresh cup and savored the smell before taking a sip. Already, he felt more human.

Wandering down to the river, he found a suitable rock and took a seat. He smiled when he noticed the water bottles bobbing around in their little pool surrounded by rocks. That was pretty good thinking on Joel's part, he had to admit. With his coffee in hand, he surveyed the rest of his surroundings in the predawn light.

He was glad that he'd remembered this place and that it had worked out so well for them last night. It was a peaceful setting, and from here all seemed well with the world. He would have never guessed that life, as he knew it, was falling apart just beyond this stand of cottonwoods.

He would never wish for something this extreme to happen, of course, but a part of him couldn't help but wonder if this is what had been inevitable.

In his opinion, America as a whole had gone astray years ago and seemed to be getting worse with every passing day. Society, as of late, seemed to be lacking a moral compass and there was really nothing in the news or online that surprised him anymore.

He felt like Americans had gone overboard in their attempt to include, congratulate, and accept everyone for everything regardless of actual effort. Both political parties at this point were complete frauds and sellouts to the highest corporate bidders. It was pretty much common knowledge to the average American citizen that politics were bought and sold. And power was traded like a commodity. The vote Americans cast come election time was merely for show at this point. Not that it mattered, as the candidates to choose from seemed to be getting worse, too.

This disaster was a reckoning for this country. People would be forced to get back to basics. Some would survive and eventually learn to thrive in this new world, and some just wouldn't make it. This would be the great equalizer, and money would no longer matter. One thing would still remain, though, and that would be the battle between good and evil in this world. They had seen this struggle firsthand and been up close and personal with it a few times yesterday. That wasn't about to change anytime soon, either.

Ben was optimistic for the day, however, and really felt like once the roads opened up it would be smoother sailing. They would try to gas up at more remote service stations not so close to towns or more inhabited areas.

They were self-sufficient, and as far as he was concerned, there was no need to interact with anyone at this point, although he would love to get some information about what was going on. He was going to have to look at the map tonight, but he knew there were some large cities along the route, and based on their experiences so far, it would be best to avoid them. If there was a reasonable way around that wouldn't add days to the trip, it would be worth the effort. The places they had been through had been small rural towns, and they had all been in rough shape.

He could only imagine the chaos that was taking place in the big cities right now. Getting Allie into Pittsburgh and finding her dad was going to be tougher than he thought. He tried to put it out of his mind for the time being; they had a lot more miles to cover before they had to deal with Pittsburgh.

Even so, it was hard not to think about it. Most of those people would only have a few days of food on hand, if even that, and without modern conveniences, they would be lost and desperate. Ben knew what desperate people were capable of, and it wasn't pretty. The big cities would be extremely dangerous, especially in the ones that had enacted strict gun laws. Outside of law enforcement, the only people that would have weapons in those places would be criminals and the worst elements of society. He was sure it would be gang rule in the inner cities for a while, at least until the government intervened.

At some point, the U.S. government would bring home all of its assets from abroad. In fact, Ben didn't doubt it was already in the works. He imagined somewhere along their journey they would encounter some National Guard troops—or at least he hoped they would.

He had read some articles about the new administration ramping up efforts to deal with a potential EMP threat. The military was supposed to start implementing some defense mechanisms against an attack of that nature, but that was a recent development and he had no idea what had been done so far. What percentage of the military, or the government for that matter, was even operational?

Someone was going to have to maintain law and order to keep society from a total meltdown, if it wasn't too late in some parts already. Regardless of when or if that happened, he knew it would be every man for himself until things settled down.

He was glad the ex lived on the Eastern Shore of Maryland and in a fairly rural area. But still, they would have to get by D.C. and straight through Baltimore. Ben wasn't fond of either city and hoped they could stick to the expressway, maybe make a late-night or early-morning run through both places. What he'd seen and read about Baltimore before the attack was enough to know it would be a lawless wasteland now.

· 21 ·

Ben was deep in thought and didn't notice Allie walking up behind him until she was only a few feet away.

"Good morning." She smiled and sipped from her mug.

"Morning," Ben replied.

"Thanks for making coffee. Hope you don't mind," she said.

Ben shook his head. "No, of course not. Help yourself."

Allie found a small rock a few feet away and sat, staring out over the river as the rising sun sparkled off the water. "It's so peaceful here."

"Yes, it is," Ben agreed.

Just then, Joel strolled down the bank with Gunner close behind. Joel had his fly rod in one hand and a cup of coffee in the other. "Good morning!"

"You're in a good mood and up early. I didn't realize we were expecting snow today," Ben joked.

"Very funny. I'm just glad I get to do a little fishing." Joel smiled as he walked past Ben and sat his coffee on a rock next to Allie.

"Do you mind watching that while I catch our breakfast?" he asked Allie.

"Nope."

"Thanks." He waded into the river up to his knees before stopping to get his fly ready. He pulled a little line off the reel and started casting as he slowly worked his way upstream, picking his steps carefully from rock to rock.

Gunner waded along, parallel to Joel, a few feet off the shoreline in chest-high water and watched the boy intently.

A few minutes in and one of Joel's casts resulted in a hooked trout that jumped with a splash some 20 yards from where Joel stood. He struggled against the fish for a few minutes before bringing it to his hand. Carefully making his way back in over the slippery rocks, he carried the trout to the bank.

"Nice Brown." Ben gave him a thumbs-up.

"Good job. Yay." Allie clapped softly.

Joel dispatched the fish quickly with a rock and laid it on the gravel.

"That's got to be at least 20 inches. And look how fat! That should be enough for everybody!" Joel beamed.

"I guess I better do my part and get breakfast going." Allie slid off the rock she was sitting on and strolled over to get a better look at the trout.

"We can help. I was thinking about making a little more coffee anyway." Ben hopped down from his spot and headed for camp.

Once Gunner realized everyone was leaving, he leapt out of the water with a splash and darted up the small pebble beach, only slowing down briefly to shake off. He went to sit under his empty food bowl that was hung upside down from a small branch where Joel had left it after rinsing it out last night. He whined anxiously.

"I'm coming, boy. Hang on." Ben, with Allie close behind, crested the river bank as it leveled out near their campsite. Joel was still down at the water's edge, cleaning the fish and getting it ready to cook.

Ben tossed Gunner's bowl on the ground and poured it half full of dry food before he started to work on boiling the water for more coffee.

Allie sorted through the food bags for a breakfast meal packet. She finally held up a bag from the back of the truck. "I've never had freeze-dried scrambled eggs before."

"Oh, well you haven't really lived until you've had freeze-dried scrambled eggs with fresh trout." Ben smiled as he walked over to the truck and looked around in the back for a second before grabbing an onion they had brought from their pantry, a small bottle of olive oil, salt, and pepper.

"Better use it while it's good." Ben put the ingredients in a small pan, then headed for the stove.

A few seconds later, Joel strolled into camp with the freshly cleaned fish.

"You can put that right in here." Ben held out the now empty and oiled pan.

"So what's the plan for today?" Joel picked up the pot of boiling water by the rubber-coated handle and poured it into the freeze-dried egg pouch that Allie had ready for him.

That freed up the little stove for the pan.

Ben got the trout cooking before he answered. "I'd love to get at least halfway across Kansas. Don't know if that's realistic or not, but that's my goal." He cut the onion up into small chunks as he held it in his hand, throwing them in the pan as he went.

"It took my mom and me three days when we drove out from Pittsburgh." Allie unzipped her fleece. "But we stopped a lot, and of course it wasn't...you know." She looked around.

"Yeah." Joel nodded. They all understood what she meant.

The fierce Colorado sun was in full glory and already warming things up. By the time they were finishing breakfast, it was actually starting to get hot, and everyone had shed a layer or two of clothing.

"After we clean up and get the gear packed, we should top off the water before we leave." Ben stood and drained the rest of the water out of his Nalgene with one gulp. "Like your little setup with the water, by the way." Ben nodded at Joel.

"Thanks." Joel smiled.

It didn't take long to break down camp with everyone pitching in and packing up. It was all loaded back in the truck within 15 minutes, and they were just about ready to leave except for a few odds and ends.

Joel and Allie walked down to the river to retrieve the water bottles and top off the empty ones. Gunner ran after them as if he knew this was his last chance to sneak in a quick swim.

Ben shook his head and called after them. "Better keep him dry. I don't think Allie wants to ride next to a wet dog, and I know I don't want to be stuck in the truck with one."

"Definitely not. We'll watch him." Joel nodded and turned back around to join Allie as they walked.

Ben leaned against the truck with his arms crossed. He tilted his head back and looked at the sky while he waited for them to return. The air seemed to be a little cleaner today and the sky actually looked a semi-normal shade of blue. The lack of jet trails and small planes flying overhead was noticeable, though, and it was almost too quiet. It would have been more enjoyable if the reason behind the empty skies and quietness wasn't so calamitous.

Ben saw Gunner galloping toward the truck as he crested the sand and gravel berm between the river and the campsite. Joel and Allie followed close behind.

"Load up." Ben opened the passenger door on the truck. Gunner launched himself into the truck without breaking stride, then sat on the front seat and waited for Joel and Allie to catch up.

"Come on, boy, all the way back." Ben sternly pointed toward the back of the truck until Gunner gave in and hopped over the console, taking his place on the rear bench seat. Ben climbed in next and joined Gunner on the rear seat. He'd decided to let Joel drive for a while this morning.

He was somewhat familiar with the next few hours' worth of road and didn't expect much trouble this early in the morning. Most of the road was a lot of long straight stretches in farmland and open range down through the foothills. Other than the scattered wrecks on the road, with any luck it should be a pretty boring drive. Besides, this would give him a chance to fool with the radio a bit more and study the map a little.

After the next couple of hours, the road ahead

would be unknown territory to him, and he had no real knowledge of the places they would be traveling through. He'd only made the drive once before, and in a hurry to get to Maryland, he hadn't paid much attention to the places they passed through.

Being in unfamiliar territory would put them at a disadvantage, so he figured the least he could do was go over the map and get to know the route a little. Maybe he could even plan some alternatives in case they ran into trouble. He would mainly focus on finding a route around Kansas City. That would be the first major city they would have to deal with, and he was determined to find a way around that wouldn't add a lot of time to the trip.

Some of the more populated areas and cities would be unavoidable the closer to Maryland they got, and as the density of people and towns increased, so did their risk for trouble. Ben knew this, and it weighed heavily on his mind.

He heard Joel and Allie talking a few seconds before he saw them come over the little hill. Joel was fixated on Allie or their conversation and didn't notice Ben was in the back until he was at the passenger door.

"I guess I'm driving?" Joel pointed at himself.

"If you don't mind," Ben replied. "It'll give me a chance to go over the map and try to figure out a good spot for tonight. I can take over at the next fuel stop if you get tired."

"No problem. I can drive all day if you want me to." Joel shrugged and handed Ben a few cold water bottles still dripping from the river.

"Here you go, Mr. Davis. I have some, too." Allie handed him bottles she was carrying.

Joel walked around to the driver's side and got in while Allie situated herself in the passenger's seat. As Ben was wrapping the water bottles up in a blanket for insulation, a thought crossed his mind—something he hadn't considered up until now.

If anything were to happen to him, would these two kids in the front seat be able to make it on their own?

Find out about Bruno Miller's next book by signing up for his newsletter:
http://brunomillerauthor.com/sign-up/

No spam, no junk, just news (sales, freebies, and releases). Scouts honor.

Enjoy the book?
Help the series grow by telling a friend about it
and taking the time to leave a review.

ABOUT THE AUTHOR

BRUNO MILLER is the author of the Dark Road series. He's a military vet who likes to spend his downtime hanging out with his wife and kids, or getting in some range time. He believes in being prepared for any situation.

http://brunomillerauthor.com/

https://www.facebook.com/BrunoMillerAuthor/

Made in the USA
Middletown, DE
23 September 2024